INTERNET GIRLS SERIES

New York Times bestselling series
San Francisco Chronicle bestselling series
Publishers Weekly bestselling series

School Library Journal:
★ Both revealing and innovative, this novel will inspire
teens to pass it to their friends . . . nonnarrative
communication can be a great way to tell a story.

Publishers Weekly:
Myracle's approach is creative . . .
an engaging quick read . . . readers will cheer.

Booklist:
Myracle cleverly manages to build rich characters
and narrative tension without ever taking the story outside
of an IM box.

Kirkus Reviews:
A surprisingly poignant tale of friendship, change, and
growth. Perfectly contemporary. ROTFL.

Teen magazine:
. . . read.

LAUREN MYRACLE

ttyl

AMULET BOOKS · NEW YORK

Cataloging-in-Publication Data has been applied for and may be obtained from the Library of Congress.

56517013
06/15

ISBN: 978-1-4197-1142-8

Text copyright © 2004, 2014 Lauren Myracle
Book design by Maria T. Middleton

Printed and bound in U.S.A.
10 9 8 7 6 5 4 3 2 1

Amulet Books are available at special discounts when purchased in quantity for premiums and promotions as well as fundraising or educational use. Special editions can also be created to specification. For details, contact specialsales@abramsbooks.com or the address below.

ABRAMS
THE ART OF BOOKS SINCE 1949

115 West 18th Street
New York, NY 10011
www.abramsbooks.com

For Erica Finkel, the hippest gal in town

SnowAngel: hey, mads! first day of 10th grade down the tube—
wh-hoo!

mad maddie: hiyas, angela. wh-hoo to you too. and yr FB post
made me laugh. that pic of u, me, and zoe at the
beach with our arms around each other? perfect,
perfect, perfect—tho of course it made me sad.

SnowAngel: did u get the daisy i put in your locker? 🌷

mad maddie: i did, and *that* made me happy

mad maddie: what's the story?

SnowAngel: i just know that the end of the summer always
throws u into a funk, so i wanted to do something to
defunkify u.

mad maddie: u wanted to DEFUNKIFY me?

SnowAngel: so that's why i gave u the daisy, to remind u of the
beach, and also our park picnics and hanging
out at the pool and going to tuckaway with zoe's
parents. happy, smiley, daisy kinda stuff, u know?

mad maddie: oh. well, thx.

SnowAngel: cuz even tho school's started, nothing has to
change. u, me, and zoe—we're gonna have a
great year. 😁

mad maddie: r we?

mad maddie: i'm already depressed just from watching
everyone compare tans.

SnowAngel: why did that depress u? ur brown as a berry.

mad maddie: all day long there was far too much squealing
going on, too much "ooo, u look fabulous!" and
"it's SO good to see u!"

SnowAngel: why is that bad?

mad maddie: cuz it's so fake. all that clique stuff, i hate it.
i hate feeling like everyone knows the secret
handshake but me.

SnowAngel:	at least u and zoe r in the same homeroom. i am insanely jealous. *shakes fist at sky*
mad maddie:	**i'll see you in math, tho. whoopee.**
SnowAngel:	and thank god all three of us have the same lunch period. *raises champagne glass* TO THE WINSOME THREESOME! BFF!
mad maddie:	**cheers!**
SnowAngel:	anyway, it doesn't matter how many secret handshakes pop up, cuz we'll always have each other. unlike susie smith—did u hear? all summer she hung out with catherine and leigh at the piedmont driving club, but now that school's started, leigh and catherine have totally dumped her.
mad maddie:	**what a pisser. susie must be heartbroken.**
SnowAngel:	come on, it would suck to have your friends drop u like that. supposedly leigh wrote an entire blog post about how susie needs to shave her pubes. isn't that awful?
mad maddie:	**have u read it?**
SnowAngel:	and catherine tweeted the condensed version. so uncool.
SnowAngel:	(read the tweet. L's blog post? too long.)
mad maddie:	**too LONG? just like susie's pubes?**
mad maddie:	**my brother's new girlfriend doesn't shave her pits OR her pubes. he brought her to this family party at lake lanier last weekend, and she wore a bikini.**
SnowAngel:	that's sick
mad maddie:	**it was basically like she had a pelt. the pops pulled me aside and said in this really loud whisper, "guess she forgot to mow the lawn, huh?"**
SnowAngel:	SICK!!!
mad maddie:	**he was drunk, of course**
SnowAngel:	i could NEVER not shave my pubes. that is just gross. but even if i did have a pubic hair problem, which i do not, u and zoe would still luv me, right?

mad maddie: hmm . . .

SnowAngel: i just mean we would never turn on each other for something stupid.

mad maddie: no, just for something un-stupid.

SnowAngel: i'm serious! ppl always say that high school friendships don't last, but we're gonna prove them wrong.

mad maddie: right on, sister

SnowAngel: remember the first day of junior high, when we all got put in the same PE class? and we had to do that horrible president's fitness dealie, and ms. cahill made me do the flexed arm hang even·tho i told her i totally couldn't?

mad maddie: that wasn't on the first day. that was like a month into the semester.

SnowAngel: and my arms gave out before she counted to three. it was so humiliating. and everybody laughed except u and zoe.

mad maddie: cuz we are true blue 🖤 🖤 🖤

SnowAngel: that's right. and we'll STAY true blue forever and ever. we'll all three go to the same college and fall in love with awesome guys who are also best friends, and we'll be bridesmaids in each other's weddings and live happily ever after. *sigh*

mad maddie: whatevs. but i'm not wearing pink, even for u.

mad maddie: g2g, the moms is yelling her head off for me to come to dinner.

SnowAngel: first u have to say it: maddie, angela, and zoe— together forever!

mad maddie: er, maddie, angela, and zoe . . . what was that last part?

SnowAngel: *glares*

mad maddie: i'm kidding, i'm kidding. but i don't HAVE to say it, angela, cuz it's true no matter what. don't make me get all mushy.

SnowAngel:	atta girl, mads. see u tomorrow!

Tues, Sept 7, 6:01 PM E.D.T.

zoegirl:	angela, thank u for the daisy!!! that was SO sweet.
SnowAngel:	zoe! u found it—yay!
zoegirl:	i was all overwhelmed with first-day madness, and then i opened my locker, and voila!
SnowAngel:	i gave one to maddie too. they're to remind us not to get caught up in stupid school stuff. we've just got to be ourselves and have as much fun as possible. 👍
zoegirl:	well, it totally made me smile.
SnowAngel:	a fabulous start to a fabulous year. and it *is* gonna be fabulous—i can feel it. i'm gonna meet the boy of my dreams, maddie's gonna stop being so down on herself all the time, and ur gonna . . . huh. what r u gonna do? ur already perfect.
zoegirl:	what?!! hardly
SnowAngel:	ok, then what's your goal for sophomore year? AND DON'T SAY STRAIGHT A'S, CUZ I'M NOT TALKING ABOUT SCHOOL.
zoegirl:	my goal?
zoegirl:	i have no idea
SnowAngel:	well, think of something
zoegirl:	i guess . . .
zoegirl:	i guess i just want something meaningful to happen. something BIG. my life is so boring compared to yours and maddie's. for once i want something exciting to happen, and i want to be the one it happens to.
SnowAngel:	yeah, baby. i can groove to that.
SnowAngel:	but u'll have to MAKE it happen. u can't just sit back and be good little zoe like u usually r.

zoegirl:	that's my point. i want to STOP being good little zoe. i want to try out whatever comes along.
SnowAngel:	excellent plan, just as long as it doesn't involve going to the sit 'n' snip. promise?
zoegirl:	silly. your haircut looks great.
SnowAngel:	right. i hate my hair! 😡 even my mom was like, "well it's not the most flattering cut u've ever had, but it'll grow out."
SnowAngel:	i always get these grand ideas of "oh, this style will be perfect," and then afterward, all i wanna do is go back in time to the good ol' days of ponytails and braids. but noooooo, it's too late, and now i'm in clippie hell till it grows out.
zoegirl:	please. you couldn't look bad if you tried.
SnowAngel:	if i wore a t-shirt that said, "i got my hair cut at sit 'n' snip," i'd put them out of business in an hour.
zoegirl:	angela, angela, angela. do you remember last year when you hennaed your hair? only, mary kate thought you said hint a', like just a hint a' red, not too much and not too little? and she went to walmart to buy some and was SO bummed when they didn't have any?
SnowAngel:	yr point . . . ?
zoegirl:	that even though you hated your henna look, everyone else wanted to steal it for their own. mary kate's going to show up tomorrow in a jillion clippies, just wait and see.
SnowAngel:	ha. ur so full of it.
zoegirl:	anyway, must stop chatting. i've got to read three chapters of "The Great Gatsby" by tomorrow.
SnowAngel:	the horror! 💀
zoegirl:	thanks again for the daisy!!!

Wed, Sept 8, 8:14 PM E.D.T.

SnowAngel: zoe! ROB TYLER is in my French class!!! *breathes deeply, with hand to throbbing bosom*

SnowAngel: on friday we have to do "une dialogue" together. i get to ask for a bite of his hot dog.

zoegirl: you do not

SnowAngel: yes, and it will be tres sexy. he is SO cute, zoe. today he was wearing this yellow button-down that was quite unexpected on a retro boy like him. he had the sleeves rolled up, and i'm telling u, he's got the greatest forearms.

zoegirl: does he, now?

SnowAngel: it's from doing construction work all summer. isn't that cool that he worked construction? it's so . . . manly.

zoegirl: you two actually talked?

SnowAngel: our seats are right next to each other. and tonight when i do my hw, i get to fantasize about his summer sausage. *nudge, nudge, wink, wink*

zoegirl: while i'll be reading 5,000 pages of "The Great Gatsby" and answering probing discussion questions about the american dream. mr. h expects us to read a book a week. can you believe that?

SnowAngel: like that'll be a problem for u.

SnowAngel: did he stare at your boobs?

zoegirl: mr. h?!

SnowAngel: maddie and i had him for journalism last year, and he was always staring at some girl's boobs, mostly maddie's. he was always "reading" her shirts.

zoegirl: ewww!

SnowAngel: so watch out. he makes a big deal of being all christian, but what that MEANS is that he's majorly sexually repressed. whereas i, on the other hand, am not sexually repressed at all. speaking of, better start practicing for rob. bye!

mad maddie: i hear angela's selected her first crush of the season.

zoegirl: rob tyler?

mad maddie: she's so funny. it's like she's got to have a guy to like, or she can't exist. it drives me batty.

zoegirl: well, that's angela

zoegirl: is rob a worthy candidate? i've never had a class with him.

mad maddie: i guess he's nice enough, in a slouchy, hipster-boy kinda way. but i must say, he's got a weak chin.

zoegirl: oh yikes! he kind of does!

mad maddie: i know angela thinks he's hot, but he reminds me of that creepy weird brother in "arrested development." NOT a good thing.

mad maddie: that show, however, will never grow old

zoegirl: think he'll fall for her?

mad maddie: they always do, don't they?

zoegirl: but then things never end up working out. why?

mad maddie: cuz every new guy is, like, a god to her. she puts them on this total pedestal, and then they do something crappy and she falls apart. and WE have to pick up the pieces.

zoegirl: well, let's not forget the time you fell deeply and madly in love with grier snelling . . .

mad maddie: hold on, now—i was in the 7th grade!!!

zoegirl: and you sent him that perfumed letter for valentine's day, only you were too chicken to put your name on it, and he was like, "ew, my desk stinks! ew, who put this here?!"

mad maddie: thx for bringing up such a joyous memory. i was scarred for life, thank u very much.

zoegirl: but angela and i put you back together, because that's what friends do. and if we have to, you and i will do the same for her.

Thu, Sept 9, 7:46 PM E.D.T.

mad maddie: i am SOOOO pissed.

SnowAngel: oh no. why?

mad maddie: one word. well, two. JANA WHITAKER.

SnowAngel: the queen bee of our entire class? *gasps* what'd she do this time?

mad maddie: i hate her. she's evil.

SnowAngel: i KNOW that. TELL ME WHAT SHE DID!!!!

mad maddie: we had a substitute for last period study hall and he insisted on taking roll, cuz god forbid one of us had snuck off to do something productive. when he got to me he called out, "madeleine kinnick?" and jana turns around, all batting eyes and innocent, and goes, "um, isn't your name madigan?"

SnowAngel: yr name IS madigan.

mad maddie: which jana totally knows!

SnowAngel: so what's the problem?

mad maddie: r u serious?!!

mad maddie: it was the way she said it, like she was honestly confused. like, "oh my goodness, i THINK i know u, don't i?" WHEN WE'VE GONE TO SCHOOL TOGETHER SINCE 7th GRADE!!!

SnowAngel: oooooh.

SnowAngel: i can see how that would be annoying.

mad maddie: it's like she thinks she's so much better than all the rest of us, and she's doing us a favor if she remembers our names. it bugs the hell out of me how she walks down the halls in her too-small shirts, her belly-button ring shouting, "look how cool i am! worship me! adore me!" as if she's such a rebel just cuz she pierced her navel.

SnowAngel: as if piercings are *any* sign of badass-ness anymore. margie walker pierced her tongue, and no one cared. oh, and she dyed her hair blue.

8

SnowAngel:	(personally, don't think it looks that great)
SnowAngel:	but jana whitaker pierces her belly button, and everyone wants to run out and copy her so they can be little jana clones.
mad maddie:	**i know. pathetic.**
SnowAngel:	anyway, jana's totally backstabbing margaret cheney. did u know that?
mad maddie:	**exsqueeze me?**
SnowAngel:	it almost makes me feel sorry for margaret, cuz she and jana r supposed to be best buds. but it's margaret's fault for trusting jana in the first place.
mad maddie:	**explain**
SnowAngel:	i was in the bathroom after 5th period. jana and terri were there, and jana was going on about what a bitch margaret was for flirting with rex saunders. i guess rex is like jana's property cuz they went to some party together over the summer.
SnowAngel:	jana was all, "she is such a whore," and then she lowered her voice like she was telling some big secret and said something REALLY gross.
mad maddie:	**and that wld be . . . ?**
SnowAngel:	don't think i can say
mad maddie:	**say.**
SnowAngel:	well, she said that margaret . . . er . . . ejaculates.
mad maddie:	**????!!!**
SnowAngel:	actually she said she squirts when she comes. and then she was like, "shit, i can't believe i told u. u've gotta swear not to tell, terri. u've gotta swear!" while the whole time i was two sinks over going, "HELLO! do u even know i'm here?"
mad maddie:	**disgusting**
SnowAngel:	i know. i was like, "margaret is yr friend, asshole. how wld u like it if she went around spreading rumors about u?"

mad maddie:	**i meant the other part. about margaret.**
SnowAngel:	oh
SnowAngel:	some girls really do, tho. i read it in "our bodies, ourselves."
mad maddie:	**ick**
SnowAngel:	not NECESSARILY. i wldn't know, but if it's just biology . . .
SnowAngel:	it's not *necessarily* ick, is it?
mad maddie:	**does jana truly NOT know my name? is that possible?**
SnowAngel:	if so, it's her loss.
mad maddie:	**it made me feel so loser-ish. christine and amber giggled when she said it, and i wanted to crawl under my desk. not that they would have noticed, since to them i'm totally invisible.**
SnowAngel:	ur not invisible, not to the ppl who matter.
SnowAngel:	hey! *lightbulb binging in head* want me to bring u some krispy kremes to cheer u up?
mad maddie:	**YEAH!**
SnowAngel:	ok, only i'll have to wait for mom to get back so she can give me a ride.
mad maddie:	**nvm. in that case i'd rather just sulk.**
SnowAngel:	poor sad maddie. i can't wait till we get our licenses. then we can do stuff like that whenever we want.
mad maddie:	**four weeks and a day for yrs truly. 🎂**
mad maddie:	**now if only i could get the moms to buy me that jeep . . .**
SnowAngel:	dream on. maybe your grandmom's old gremlin . . .
mad maddie:	**the gremlin OWNS. it runs, anywayz.**
mad maddie:	**wanna hear my post-driving-test fantasy?**
SnowAngel:	i dunno. do i?
mad maddie:	**it's probably impossible, but wldn't it be awesome if u, me, and zoe cld go on a road trip together, just the three of us?**

SnowAngel: omg, that would be so cool.

mad maddie: crank up the music, roll down the windows, and just GO.

SnowAngel: we cld drive to tuckaway. or hilton head! we cld be beach blanket bimbos! 😎

mad maddie: and we cld get away from everything having to do with school. we cld just leave it all behind us.

SnowAngel: that would be so awesome.

SnowAngel: SHIT, maddie, why do u put these ideas in my head? now i totally wanna do it!

mad maddie: but the rents will never let us. well, mine might if i begged hard enough, cuz they don't give a shit what i do. but yours and zoe's wld freak out.

SnowAngel: i know. that so sucks.

mad maddie: one day, tho . . .

SnowAngel: well, i call shotgun on our first krispy kreme run.

mad maddie: u got it!

Thu, Sept 9, 8:25 PM E.D.T.

SnowAngel: maddie told me what happened in study hall. was jana really out to humiliate maddie, or is maddie just being dramatic?

zoegirl: maddie? dramatic? hahahahaha

SnowAngel: but did jana really say all that, like jana didn't even know maddie's name?

zoegirl: yeah, only . . . i don't know. i think jana just wanted to straighten out the sub without technically correcting him.

SnowAngel: oh

zoegirl: don't tell maddie i said that, though. she gets so weird when it comes to jana and that crowd.

SnowAngel: it's that whole stupid in-crowd thing. it's so not fair. the nice ppl—like US—should be the popular ones. then we'd have all the power, but we'd use it in a good way. like if jana made some snide remark about someone's kmart clothes, we cld bitch-slap her till she apologized.

zoegirl: oh definitely. me, the b*tch-slapper.

SnowAngel: and the next time she slammed someone's reputation—remember when she "let it slip" about heidi larson's shoplifting charge?—we cld dig up some dirt on her and post it online. then she'd know what it felt like.

zoegirl: i guess

zoegirl: i've got a conference with mr. h tomorrow, and i'm supposed to make a list of possible essay topics. i want to make a good impression, so off i go. bye!

Thu, Sept 9, 9:05 PM E.D.T.

mad maddie: **did they say anything else?**

SnowAngel: who?

mad maddie: **jana and terri, when u were in the bathroom with them.**

SnowAngel: no, except jana did mention how excited she was to be in homeroom with madeleine kinnick. JK!!!!

mad maddie: **ur a laugh riot**

SnowAngel: i know 😬

SnowAngel: seriously, maddie, jana is SO not worth your time. stop letting it get to u!

Fri, Sept 10, 8:51 PM E.D.T.

mad maddie: **hey, babe. how was your meeting with mr. h?**

zoegirl: it was good. it was kind of cool, actually, because after we talked about my paper, we talked about other things. like religion and stuff.

mad maddie: **in other words he stared at your boobs and lectured u about the sins of the body?**

zoegirl: no!

zoegirl: that's not at *all* what happened.

mad maddie: when i had him for journalism last year, he was always having girls stay late for "conferences." once he made jody fisher stay late and do the skirt-length test, like did her fingers reach farther than the bottom of it when she held her hands to her sides.

zoegirl: i have a really hard time believing that.

zoegirl: or if he did, he was probably just trying to watch out for her. like he didn't want her to get busted for breaking the dress code.

mad maddie: she said he got a total stiffie while they were talking. she said it was hysterical.

zoegirl: that's ridiculous. mr. h would never do that.

mad maddie: what makes u so sure?

zoegirl: because he's NICE. because he treats me like i'm a person instead of a kid. that's what was so great during our meeting—we were just two people having a discussion.

mad maddie: what did the two of u "discuss"?

zoegirl: NOT skirt lengths or anything like that. geez. we both said how we believe there's meaning to life, that everything's not random and pointless like some people think. mr. h talked about christianity a little—how he's sure God has a plan for him. he told me that everything that happens, happens for a reason. doesn't that give you the chills?

mad maddie: yesterday at publix, a little kid rammed me with a grocery cart. was there a message there? cuz i think i missed it.

zoegirl: he also said that sometimes you'll meet someone totally unexpected and it'll change your life in a way you can't even imagine. now that really gave me the chills.

mad maddie: zoe. do u even hear what ur saying?

zoegirl: what?

mad maddie: "it'll change your life in a way u can't even imagine"? he is hitting on u!!!

zoegirl: shut up. just because you can't be serious, that doesn't mean no one else can.

zoegirl: it was a good conversation. it felt . . . important.

mad maddie: whatevs. i still say he's hitting on u!

Fri, Sept 10, 9:19 PM E.D.T.

mad maddie: i'm listening to the Contemporary Christian station on Pandora in your honor. thought u should know.

zoegirl: yeah right

mad maddie: it's giving me warm JC fuzzines, baby!

Sun, Sept 12, 8:52 PM E.D.T.

SnowAngel: aarrghhh! 😠

zoegirl: hello to you too.

SnowAngel: aarrghhhhhhh!

zoegirl: something bothering you?

SnowAngel: chrissy dropped my face brush into the toilet!!!

zoegirl: huh?

SnowAngel: my hinoki polishing facial brush—IN THE TOILET!!!
stomps on picture of chrissy

zoegirl: you brush your face?

SnowAngel: yr missing the point. my sister dropped my face brush into the toilet, which was, yes, currently in use. by HER. the toilet, not my face brush.

SnowAngel: well, actually both

SnowAngel: AND she's got strep, so her pee is all orange from antibiotics. *stomp stomp stomp*

zoegirl:	i take it you're not happy about this?
SnowAngel:	would u be? i use my face brush to wash my FACE. u know, instead of a washcloth. it lifts away dead cells while improving circulation.
zoegirl:	you don't say
SnowAngel:	AND I JUST THIS VERY SECOND USED IT!!!! AFTER SHE DROPPED IT IN THE FREAKIN TOILET!!!!!!!!
zoegirl:	ewww. why?
SnowAngel:	*pulls hair from roots* cuz she didn't TELL me until just now! she thought i'd be mad!
zoegirl:	so basically you washed your face in chrissy's stinky orange pee?
SnowAngel:	u r not being helpful. *stomps on picture of zoe AND picture of chrissy*
zoegirl:	i'm sorry, but that's disgusting. surely chrissy washed it off.
SnowAngel:	she RINSED it. that's what she says, she RINSED it. like that makes me feel a hell of a lot better.
zoegirl:	back in christopher columbus's time, people used to brush their teeth with pee. did u know that?
SnowAngel:	*breathes deeply* i did not know that, zoe.
zoegirl:	although i think it was only people who were taking long sea voyages and ran out of toothpaste . . .
SnowAngel:	that's it. good-bye.
zoegirl:	wait! angela?
zoegirl:	angela!!!!
zoegirl:	fine. just don't expect me to kiss you tomorrow. air kisses, that's all you'll get!
zoegirl:	ANGELA!!!!!!

Mon, Sept 13, 5:15 PM E.D.T.

SnowAngel:	hellooo, maddie

mad maddie: hellooo, angela

SnowAngel: i saw jana whitaker after 6th period today. she was looking especially tacky in her sparkly emerald eyeshadow, and she was trash-talking julie matthews. i swear, she is ALWAYS putting down ppl who are supposedly her friends. have u noticed?

mad maddie: what'd she say?

SnowAngel: terri was like, "oh, julie, u look so cute. u cld be anna kendrick's secret twin, i'm not kidding." and jana goes, "so true! u could totally be her twin— the chubby version!"

mad maddie: ouch

SnowAngel: julie turned bright red and tugged on her shirt, like to cover herself up, and jana goes, "just stick to your diet, you'll get there." as if calling her chubby was ok since it was mixed in with this great show of support. but julie's not even fat, so there was no reason for jana to say all that in the first place.

mad maddie: does jana have a reason for anything she says?

SnowAngel: i swear, she's like an infection. she gloms on wherever she spots a weakness and makes it five thousand times worse.

mad maddie: and yet everyone still worships her and secretly craves her approval. why is that?

SnowAngel: i have NO idea. anyway, not everyone craves her approval. i certainly don't. and u don't, of course.

SnowAngel: right?

mad maddie: please. this morning ms. andrist lectured me about being tardy, and i could tell jana was laughing about it behind my back. i can always tell. it's like i have jana radar. so i gave her the evil eye and was like, "yeah? u want some of this, homegirl?"

SnowAngel: good for u, homegirl. *flicks jana off the stage*

mad maddie: what about u and rob? how's that going?

SnowAngel: oh, pah. u know how i told u that today was the day i was gonna make my move? well, he sat next to me in french, and i acted totally blase. just, "hey, rob." no real excitement in my voice or anything.

mad maddie: why? at lunch u were like, "watch out, bubba. here i come."

SnowAngel: i know, so what's my deal? i need to help him along as much as possible, or else forget about him. i get so mad at myself when i act disinterested around guys i like.

mad maddie: yes, it's a real trauma

SnowAngel: it is!

SnowAngel: oh, hold on. doug schmidt just sent me a txt—let me txt him back real quick.

SnowAngel: ok, done

mad maddie: doug still texts you? what did he want this time?

SnowAngel: to know if i wanted to go bike riding. i told him i was sick, but i don't think he believed me.

mad maddie: hmm, wonder why. maybe cuz u've rejected him once a week for the past two years?

SnowAngel: well, he shld take the hint!

SnowAngel: uh oh—now he wants to know if he should bring me some chicken soup. what shld i tell him?

mad maddie: the truth. that he's simply not in your league and he should aim his sights lower.

SnowAngel: maddie! *gazes at friend reproachfully* u make me sound awful.

mad maddie: well think about how it sounds: oh no, a guy asked me out! how terrible! and now he wants to bring me get-well gifts!

SnowAngel: stop it. i hate turning doug down again and again. but isn't it better to do that than to lead him on?

mad maddie: are u sure yr NOT still leading him on?

SnowAngel:	there, i told doug VERY NICELY that i don't need any soup cuz i look too terrible to come to the door. r u happy?
mad maddie:	**"very nicely?" uh huh. point proven.**
SnowAngel:	oh god. AM i awful? am i shallow and self-centered cuz i don't wanna go out with doug?
mad maddie:	**yes**
SnowAngel:	maddie! now i'm all paranoid
SnowAngel:	i know. maybe i'll call doug later just to chat, so he'll know i'm not a jerk. but i'll chat about boring stuff so he knows i'm not interested THAT WAY. and then afterward i'll call rob and turn on the ol' charm, so that he'll know that i *am* interested that way.
mad maddie:	**ur hopeless. it's official.**

Mon, Sept 13, 5:45 PM E.D.T.

SnowAngel:	OMG!!!
mad maddie:	**what?!**
SnowAngel:	i called rob, just like i said i would, and he asked me out! for TONIGHT!!! 😶
mad maddie:	**damn, girl. u r good.**
SnowAngel:	he's taking me out to dinner, and then we're going to some party at kyle's.
SnowAngel:	hey, u could come if u want—u and zoe both! not to the dinner part, obviously, but rob says kyle's party is gonna be huge.
mad maddie:	**kyle's having a party on a monday night?**
SnowAngel:	his parents r out of town, but they're coming back on wednesday, so this is the only night he can do it. come!
mad maddie:	**yeah, that's what i wanna do—have the moms drop me off at kyle's in front of the whole friggin grade. with my luck jana would be there laughing her head off.**

SnowAngel:	I CAN'T BELIEVE I HAVE A DATE WITH ROB! MUST GO PRIMP! 💄 🤚 💜

Tues, Sept 14, 4:15 PM E.D.T.

SnowAngel:	zoe! dahling!
zoegirl:	you better be texting to tell me about your madcap night with rob. you can't put me off any longer!!!
SnowAngel:	he was sitting RIGHT BEHIND US, zoe. what did u want me to do, announce to his face how in love with him i am?
zoegirl:	it was the cafeteria. we were at separate tables. AND, if you were afraid to use your words like a big girl, guess what? you could have texted me then just like you're texting me now. hmmm?
SnowAngel:	and break the no-phones-allowed-during-class rule? *draws hand to mouth*
zoegirl:	TELL ME!!!
SnowAngel:	ok. me: long-sleeve white shirt, slightly tattered miniskirt, platform wedges, silver square bracelet, garnet ring. hair down. him: "moab" t-shirt, jeans, those overly huge sneakers boys seem genetically wired to wear. adorable sticky-uppy hair.
zoegirl:	very nice, although i'm not sure i agree about his hair. i'm thinking it's more lack of hygiene than stylistic flair.
zoegirl:	where'd you go for dinner?
SnowAngel:	bennigan's. mmmm. and while we were waiting for our food, he told this hysterical story about this time he called the home shopping network. did u know the home shopping network even existed still? well, it does.
SnowAngel:	they were selling a watch that was supposedly indestructible, and rob phoned in and asked, "yes,

	but does it resist cheese dip?" only he pronounced it really funny, like che-e-e-ese dip.
zoegirl:	i wish i knew how to tell funny stories. i always get embarrassed and start mumbling, and then i wish i'd never started.
SnowAngel:	then he said, "cuz my last watch stopped working when i dropped it in a bowl of che-e-e-ese dip. so tell me: this solid gold watch u've got on the screen there, can it handle the dairy products?"
SnowAngel:	rob says they broadcast his voice and everything! god, i wish i'd heard it!
zoegirl:	what'd you do after dinner?
SnowAngel:	we went to that party at kyle's and danced the night away to patrick benson's awful garage band. well, i danced. rob kinda shifted his weight from one foot to the other.
zoegirl:	white man's boogie. did he bite his lower lip?
SnowAngel:	no, but he bit mine! 😳 later, that is, when he took me home. yippee! the boy can kiss!
zoegirl:	go, angela!
SnowAngel:	*sighs in ecstasy*
SnowAngel:	what about u? what's up in your world?
zoegirl:	nothing nearly so exciting—although you might want to talk to maddie if you haven't already.
SnowAngel:	why?
zoegirl:	because i highly doubt she wants to talk to me.
SnowAngel:	no, i meant why shld i talk to her? what happened?
zoegirl:	well, she called me up to get my opinion on this letter she'd written, and i . . . ah, crap.
SnowAngel:	what? what did u do?!
zoegirl:	i corrected her grammar
SnowAngel:	u didn't
zoegirl:	i did

SnowAngel: zoe! u know how much she hates being corrected—
                especially by you!
zoegirl: i just wanted to help!
zoegirl: and then i told her i was just being anal and to
                forget everything i'd said, and she said, "you
                don't have to lie, zoe."
SnowAngel: ouch
zoegirl: so will u talk to her?
SnowAngel: i'll txt her now.
SnowAngel: want me to report back?
zoegirl: if there's anything to report back, yes!

Tues, Sept 14, 4:33 PM E.D.T.

SnowAngel: mads! wazzup?
mad maddie: **ur interrupting a very important quiz on my**
                planetary personality. did zoe tell u to check on
                me?
SnowAngel: ???
mad maddie: **hold on, the little men in my phone are**
                processing my quiz results. wanna hear what
                planet i am?
SnowAngel: uh, sure . . . ?
mad maddie: **i scored 85% Powerful Pluto. pasting in what it**
                says:

                Although you tend to wallow in your misery, Pluto's
                energy gives you the power to change your life—if
                you dare. It may be scary, but Pluto doesn't care.
                This planet knows how to play with the big boys.

SnowAngel: i wanna play with the big boys! send me the quiz.
mad maddie: **it's at <u>helloquizzy.com/tests/what-planet-are-you-</u>**
                <u>from-test</u>. i'll forward it to zoe too.

SnowAngel:	so ur NOT mad at her. yay!
mad maddie:	**excuse me?**
SnowAngel:	oh, uh . . .
SnowAngel:	*does random hand gestures as a distraction technique*
mad maddie:	**forget it. i don't care. she told u about my pathetic letter?**
SnowAngel:	she never said it was pathetic. she's worried yr mad at her, that's all.
mad maddie:	**well, i'm not bursting with joy.**
SnowAngel:	who was the letter to? i don't get it.
mad maddie:	**if u MUST hear the whole sad story . . .**
SnowAngel:	i must
mad maddie:	**fine. chapter 1: maddie is in study hall with evil jana, who is writing notes to terri and laughing hysterically, like hahahahaha! we have a life and u don't!**
SnowAngel:	hate it when ppl do that. like they're trying to rub it in your face how much fun they're having.
mad maddie:	**chapter 2: class is dismissed and everyone goes squealing out of the room. only maddie (that's me) stupidly leaves her geometry notebook behind, so she goes back to get it. and there, lazily packing up her stuff, is jana. by herself. there is no one else around, just jana and maddie. u with me?**
SnowAngel:	uh oh . . .
mad maddie:	**chapter 3: maddie, being the kind good soul that she is, decides to say "hello." just "hello," all right? normal ppl do it all the time. AND WHAT DOES JANA DO?**
mad maddie:	**she keeps shoving books into her backpack, la-di-da, like no one is freakin there! she didn't even look up or nod or anything!**

SnowAngel: oh, that makes me so mad. that is SO ridiculous!!!

SnowAngel: but why do u even care what jana does or doesn't do?

mad maddie: chapter 4: maddie goes to snack machine and buys a king-size snickers to ease her pain. chapter 5: the snickers is rotten inside. like, really, really nasty. chapter 6: once she gets home, maddie whips off a complaint letter in a frenzy of self-righteousness. chapter 7: maddie calls zoe and reads it to her over the phone, and chapter 8: zoe makes maddie feel like total shit, as usual, which is just lovely after a day like this.

SnowAngel: oh, maddie 😟

mad maddie: i was all proud of myself, and zoe starts lecturing me on what a dumbass i am who can't even write a stupid complaint letter!

SnowAngel: she did not say u were a dumbass and u know it.

mad maddie: i just hate it that she's so good at everything and that i suck.

SnowAngel: did u tell her all the jana stuff? before u read your letter?

mad maddie: no. i was already humiliated enough, thank u very much.

SnowAngel: but zoe wouldn't care. i mean, she'd care, but in a good way.

mad maddie: yeah, well

SnowAngel: anyway, maybe jana didn't hear u. maybe that's why she didn't say hi back.

mad maddie: right. she didn't hear me when we were the only two people in the room.

SnowAngel: madikins? U R AWESOME. u want a list of all your glorious qualities?

mad maddie: no

mad maddie: yes

SnowAngel:	ur funny. ur tough. ur gorgeous and hot, even tho u never wear makeup (u really SHLD let me give u a makeover, however), and your cheekbones r freakin incredible. even my mom says so.
mad maddie:	**she does?**
SnowAngel:	she's like, "maddie is someone whose looks r only gonna improve as she gets older."
mad maddie:	**that does not sound like a compliment**
SnowAngel:	and for the record, zoe and i are both insanely jealous of your hair. ur like "lion-girl" with your tumbled golden curls.
mad maddie:	**tumbled golden curls???**
mad maddie:	**zoe is not jealous of a single part of me, even— excuse me while i gag—my "tumbled golden curls."**
SnowAngel:	we LOVE u, mads. i love u and zoe loves u, and just so u know, she really does feel bad.
mad maddie:	**whatevs. no big deal.**
SnowAngel:	so . . . ur all right?
mad maddie:	**yeah, i'm fine.**
SnowAngel:	remember, ur awesome!!! ⭐

Tues, Sept 14, 4:41 PM E.D.T.

SnowAngel:	i'm ba-a-ck
zoegirl:	hold on, giving mary kate english assignment
zoegirl:	okay, done. did you talk to maddie?
SnowAngel:	yes, and her bad mood wasn't really about u. there was the normal "zoe is so much better than me" baloney, but there was all this jana stuff going on too. so it was the totally wrong time for u to be a grammar nazi, but there's no way u could have known.
zoegirl:	eeesh
SnowAngel:	but she's fine.

zoegirl:	good. maybe i can stop worrying about her and start focusing on my english paper. i've got another meeting with mr. h tomorrow, and i really want to impress him.
SnowAngel:	no sweat. just wear a tight shirt and he'll give u an A.
zoegirl:	want to lend me one of yours?
SnowAngel:	sure! 👍
zoegirl:	i was KIDDING, angela.
SnowAngel:	hey, if u've got it, flaunt it. that's what my mom says!

Wed, Sept 15, 7:32 PM E.D.T.

SnowAngel:	hey, mads. i just had a total Zoe's Scary Mother flashback.
mad maddie:	**oh yeah? lemme put "Scandal" on pause. kk, go.**
SnowAngel:	well, i called zoe two minutes ago and accidentally INTERRUPTED THEIR DINNER. *horror movie sound effects*
SnowAngel:	even scarier? mrs. barrett answered her phone!
SnowAngel:	zoe's MOM answered zoe's phone. i'm not even kidding. she was like, "this is not an appropriate time to call, angela," and i almost peed my pants.
mad maddie:	**u shld have peed into the phone**
SnowAngel:	it reminded me of that time zoe was supposed to meet her at starbucks, but didn't. remember?
mad maddie:	**???**
SnowAngel:	zoe came home with me from school, and later she was supposed to meet her mom at the peachtree battle starbucks. but by six it was storming like crazy, and my mom was like, "zoe, u can't walk to starbucks in this weather. call your mom and tell her to pick u up here. she'll understand."
SnowAngel:	so zoe did, and her mom came to get her. but she was PISSED.

mad maddie:	**what did she do?**
SnowAngel:	she was all, "u have made me go out of my way and u have wasted my time. i expect better than this from u!"
mad maddie:	**sounds just like her**
SnowAngel:	my mom tried to step in and explain, and mrs. barrett totally ignored her. she just yanked zoe out of the house. by then it was obvious zoe was trying not to cry, and it was AWFUL.
mad maddie:	**i don't call zoe if it's anywhere NEAR dinnertime, cuz i've gotten mrs. barrett's little lecture too.**
mad maddie:	**u think that's why zoe gets so uptight sometimes? cuz her mom's so hard on her?**
SnowAngel:	well, duh. she thinks she has to be perfect cuz that's what her mom tells her every minute of the day.
SnowAngel:	thank god she has us, u know?
mad maddie:	**damn straight**
SnowAngel:	on a pleasanter subject, i took that "what planet r u" quiz. wanna hear my results?
mad maddie:	**let's have 'em**
SnowAngel:	You scored 95% Vivacious Venus. Venus is the planet of love and pleasure, and you're the poster child. You're quite the social butterfly, and few can resist your seductive moves. You rarely deny yourself any of life's pleasures, but be careful that you don't forget the benefits of hard work and self-discipline!
mad maddie:	**u? a social butterfly?**
SnowAngel:	let's not leave out my seductive moves. 😊 speaking of, i'm meeting rob at 7-11 tomorrow after school. wanna come? *slips on sock puppets and sings out loud* i love this place, my slurpee is so green!
mad maddie:	**wtf?**
SnowAngel:	hey, zo just sent me a txt. just . . . hold on. gonna start group message, brb

SnowAngel: hello, my petals.

zoegirl: hey, angela. sorry about my mom.

zoegirl: and, uh, hey, mads.

mad maddie: **hey, zo**

zoegirl: are you still mad at me from yesterday? because
. . . you kind of weren't the warmest at school.

mad maddie: **u kinda weren't either**

SnowAngel: kids, kids! hug and make up already, will you?

zoegirl: i will if maddie will

mad maddie: **all right, fine. how about this: zoe? if i want help
with my grammar—unlikely, but if—i'll come to u,
instead of the other way around. k?**

zoegirl: okay.

zoegirl: sorry again.

mad maddie: **honestly, it's all just stupid. crappy mood
yesterday, crappy mood today.**

mad maddie: ***i* think we shld change the subject. zoe, how'd yr
meeting with mr. h go today? he hit on u again?**

zoegirl: oh please

mad maddie: **did u have any Deep Discussions? did he change
the course of your life in a way u couldn't even
imagine?**

SnowAngel: what r y'all talking about? i'm lost!

zoegirl: not exactly . . . although he did invite me to come
to wellspring on friday.

SnowAngel: what's wellspring?

zoegirl: it's a church group, only not for one particular
church. it's for high school kids, and there's a
devotional and singing and stuff like that. on
fridays they meet for breakfast, and mr. h invited
me to come.

mad maddie: **it's for high school kids, but yr TEACHER invited u
to come? what did u say?**

zoegirl:	i said sure
mad maddie:	**u did not**
zoegirl:	did too. he's gonna pick me up at seven on friday morning.
mad maddie:	**zoe!!! u holy roller, u! somebody's gonna read that poem about the footprints, i can see it now.**
SnowAngel:	WHAT POEM ABOUT FOOTPRINTS? 👣
SnowAngel:	y'all are confusing me!
mad maddie:	**it's about this guy who's walking along a cliff, only it's not just him, cuz there's two sets of footprints, and somehow we know that the second pair belongs to God. yay, God!**
mad maddie:	**but then the guy gets to a really steep part, and when he looks back one of the sets is gone. oh no!**
zoegirl:	maddie. you are making fun of me.
mad maddie:	**so the guy goes, "oh, my father, why did u forsake me in my time of need?" and God says, "oh no, my son. no, no, no. i was carrying u, don't u see?"**
zoegirl:	it's sweet. and also my grandmom has a copy of that poem in her bedroom, in a big gold frame.
SnowAngel:	my grandmom has a picture of me in a big gold frame. 😇
mad maddie:	**i can't believe u said yes to mr. h. i truly can't believe it.**
zoegirl:	maddie, you're overreacting. angela, tell her.
SnowAngel:	um . . . i think i'll go play around on pinterest instead. looking for new ways to decorate my room. bye!
zoegirl:	did she really leave?
zoegirl:	angela?
mad maddie:	**she was weirded out by the inappropriate sexual conduct she was witnessing.**
zoegirl:	maddie, quit. i'm excited mr. h asked me. i wish you could be happy for me too. i mean, out of all the ppl at school, he picked *me*.

zoegirl:	it made me feel special.
mad maddie:	i thought u said lots of kids went to this shindig.
zoegirl:	yeah, but i'm the only one he's giving a ride to.
mad maddie:	whatevs. just PLEASE don't get in a back-scratching train. my brother went to this lock-in once at his friend's church, and he said that all night long everyone gave each other back scratches.
zoegirl:	i so can't see your brother at a lock-in. mark went to a lock-in?
mad maddie:	he said back-scratching trains r how christian boys cop a feel.
zoegirl:	relax, i won't get in a back-scratching train.
mad maddie:	all right, then.
mad maddie:	u take that quiz i sent u?
zoegirl:	u and your quizzes.
zoegirl:	hold on, i'll pull up my results:

You scored 75% Structured Saturn. Saturn is the planet of responsibility and discipline, and you couldn't be more reliable if you tried. While it's admirable to be so diligent and self-disciplined, know that life's too short not to break the rules every once in a while.

mad maddie:	ha! that is SO u.
zoegirl:	thanks a lot. you and angela get the fun planets, and what do i get? i get sucky saturn, planet of responsibility and discipline.
mad maddie:	hey, they call 'em as they see 'em.
zoegirl:	and who would "they" be, the planetary fairies?
mad maddie:	as opposed to the God and baby jesus fairies?
mad maddie:	jk. i really do believe in God, just not wellspring.
zoegirl:	whatever. bye, powerful pluto.
mad maddie:	byeas, structured saturn.

zoegirl: ttyl!

Wed, Sept 15, 8:40 PM E.D.T.

mad maddie: **yo, angela! come back from the Land of Pinterest!**

SnowAngel: u again! wazzup?

mad maddie: **zoe and mr. h and this friday morning fellowship thing???? u seriously think this is normal?**

SnowAngel: well, i seriously think it's . . . i dunno. it's a school-sponsored event, isn't it?

mad maddie: **is it? and even so, how does that make it better?**

mad maddie: **they're all gonna join hands and sing "It Only Takes a Spark!" you know they are.**

SnowAngel: aw, i like that song. it makes me feel all warm inside. 😃

mad maddie: **oh god**

SnowAngel: *looks soulfully into the distance* that's how it is with God's love, once u experience it. u wanna sing, it's fresh like spring, u wa-a-a-nt to pas-s-s-ss it on.

SnowAngel: i think it's called "pass it on," come to think of it.

mad maddie: **it just surprises me that zoe's getting all religious. i thought she was smarter than that.**

SnowAngel: what, smart ppl can't be religious? and zoe goes to church, u know. at least every so often.

mad maddie: **yeah . . . but friday morning fellowship????**

SnowAngel: oh, phooey. maybe she'll meet some guys.

mad maddie: **like mr. h, u mean?**

mad maddie: **a teacher shouldn't be offering rides to his students when it's just going to be the two of them. especially when it's mr. h.**

SnowAngel: relax, maddie. repeat after me: "zoe is just going to friday morning fellowship. she has not sold her soul to the devil."

mad maddie: **yeah? just u wait!**

zoegirl:	hey, angela. i called you about an hour ago—did you get my message?
SnowAngel:	yeah, sorry for not answering. i was hanging out with rob. *drools*
SnowAngel:	i actually can't txt for long cuz he's picking me up at 8 to go hear this band at the dark horse.
zoegirl:	the dark horse? isn't that a bar?
SnowAngel:	i'm gonna use his sister's i.d.
zoegirl:	you better be careful. you could get so busted if the bouncer doesn't go for it.
SnowAngel:	nah, rob says they'd just take lisa's license and cut it up, but that's not gonna happen. so what'd u call about?
zoegirl:	you know i'm going to friday morning fellowship, right?
SnowAngel:	yeah, and maddie's steamed like a pot sticker.
zoegirl:	i know. it's bizarre. it's like she thinks i'm joining some beardy-weirdy religious cult.
SnowAngel:	maybe . . . or maybe she's afraid ur gonna jump in the sack with mr. h.
zoegirl:	angela!!! please don't even SAY that. like mr. h would even consider it!
SnowAngel:	would u want him to?
zoegirl:	very funny.
zoegirl:	*i* think it has to do with the whole religious thing, and the fact that it means i'll be hanging out with new people. all day at school maddie called me her sister in christ, and then she'd throw out a word like "shit" or "balls" and gasp as if she was afraid she'd offended me. "oh dear," she'd say. "will your new friends be pissed? i mean, perturbed?"
SnowAngel:	she's just teasing

31

zoegirl:	it's so irritating. i wouldn't care if she wanted to hang out with other people.
SnowAngel:	r u kidding? i would! 4ever friends, remember? the winsome threesome?
zoegirl:	but that doesn't mean JUST us.
SnowAngel:	it doesn't? jk
zoegirl:	it's just . . . i really like talking to mr. h, that's all.
zoegirl:	i'm not going to start wearing huge crosses around my neck, and i'm not going to replace madigan with cherryl ann booth. geez.
SnowAngel:	i know. don't worry.
zoegirl:	but back to why i called. i know it's dumb, but what should i wear? to friday morning fellowship, i mean.
SnowAngel:	dumb? *widens eyes* zoe, fashion is NEVER dumb!
zoegirl:	soooo?
SnowAngel:	well, zoe dear, it's all about the details. say, for example, i'm getting ready for a date . . . hey, wait a minute! i AM getting ready for a date!
zoegirl:	go on
SnowAngel:	and say i put powder on my nose to get rid of the shininess, and i use just a dab of cheek tint to get that flushed-and-glowing look, and i curl my eyelashes for ten seconds on each side and put on one coat of black mascara, AFTER gently wiping the wand on a square of toilet paper to de-glumpify it . . .
SnowAngel:	well, say i do all that, but i forget to pluck the nasty and annoying chin hair that appears like clockwork a week before i get my period. (not that i ever wld. i HATE that chin hair.)
SnowAngel:	but say i did, do u think rob would fall to his knees and worship me for the goddess i am?
zoegirl:	um . . . is this somehow going to lead back to me? and what i should wear?
SnowAngel:	let's do a visual, shall we? *whips out artist's palette

and jaunty beret* Portrait of Zoe on a Typical Day: shiny brown hair in cute little bob, big brown eyes, shy smile.

SnowAngel: so far, so good, which is lucky since u can't do much about your basic face. u COULD flip out the ends of your hair and add some wax for an edgier look, but blah, blah, blah, i know u won't.

zoegirl: i look stupid when i try to do my hair some fancy way. we have gone over this.

SnowAngel: zoe, zoe, zoe. even Amish girls use wax, like Betsy on "Breaking Amish," remember?

zoegirl: no, because i never watched that show and i still can't believe you did.

SnowAngel: still can't believe i *do*. it's a great background show for doing hw to.

SnowAngel: but whatever, let's move on. it's a school thing, not a date, even tho it's at some guy's house. u wanna be comfy and casual, but still look good. i say u can't go wrong with jeans and a white t-shirt. NOT your dad's vanderbilt shirt, but a shirt that fits. do u own one that fits?

zoegirl: you don't think that's boring, jeans and a t-shirt?

SnowAngel: think classic, zoe. not boring. add in a pair of dangly earrings and ur good to go.

zoegirl: what about you? what are you wearing to the dark horse?

SnowAngel: well since u asked. attire: black tank, skinny jeans, my black boots with the buckles, hair in a jillion clippies. scent: Juicy. makeup: standard, but with thicker eyeliner for that over-21 look.

SnowAngel: whaddaya think?

zoegirl: lovely, dahling

SnowAngel: *kisses all around* and now i simply must run. gotta go pluck that chin hair!

SnowAngel: i'm in heaven!!! simply heaven!!!

zoegirl: hey, angela. i am SO sorry, but i was seriously just about to turn my phone off. i am soooo tired.

SnowAngel: don't u wanna hear about my romantic evening? i wld have called, but i was too scared of yo mama since it's so late.

zoegirl: can u tell me all about it tomorrow?

SnowAngel: but, zoe! i think he may be THE ONE.

zoegirl: the "one" what?

SnowAngel: *lowers voice to stage whisper* the one i go all the way with (!!!)

zoegirl: oh god

SnowAngel: i'm saying MAYBE, that's all. IF things keep going well—and i know they will. *swoons*

SnowAngel: making love with rob would be amazing, i just know it.

zoegirl: and how, exactly, do u know it?

SnowAngel: cuz he's hot! and cuz at least i've done more than kiss a guy, that's how.

SnowAngel: anyway, one of us has to go for it eventually so she can tell the others what it's like. and not to be rude, but it's not gonna be u or maddie.

zoegirl: well, now that i know ur really doing it for us . . .

SnowAngel: ☺

zoegirl: i'm just glad you're not rushing into things. i'm glad you went out on two whole dates before making this life-changing decision.

SnowAngel: rob and i have a true connection, zoe. u know i'm never wrong about these things!

SnowAngel: hey, hot stuff. i seeeeeeee u, u know.

mad maddie: well, yes. we R both in the cafeteria line. yr point?

SnowAngel: i have no point. but i also see rob, and i wld just like to say, "damn, that boy has a fine ass."

mad maddie: okay

SnowAngel: okay, what?

mad maddie: u said u wld like to say it, so say it. who's stopping u?

SnowAngel: heh?

SnowAngel: OH. haha. but, sure!

SnowAngel: damn, that boy has a fine ass! 🔥

mad maddie: u shdln't say ass. is bad word, fuckhead.

SnowAngel: if there is a roll shortage, grab me one! and a spare 🍪!

SnowAngel: and u know how much i love my butter, so grab some extra butter thingies too. ok, my little bunghole spunk-bubble?

mad maddie: *your* bunghole spunk-bubble?

mad maddie: i am no woman's spunk-bubble save my own!

SnowAngel: 😙 mwah!

Fri, Sept 17, 5:15 PM E.D.T.

mad maddie: s'up, peepz? u heading over for our friday night festivities?

zoegirl: in car with mom. there in five. was i supposed to bring anything?

mad maddie: just yo dancin ass, baby, cuz robyn is crankin and i'm ready to groove. (er, if you won't be offended, that is. she does say the f-word, u know.)

zoegirl: angela on the way too?

mad maddie: yes'm, and when we see her, we can tease her about her loverboy some more. "oh, he is so amazing. every moment at the dark horse was something special. i really think he's the one!!!"

zoegirl: you don't really think she's gonna sleep with him, do you?

mad maddie:	r u serious? she may be a fool, our angela, but she's no skank.
zoegirl:	i never said she was!
mad maddie:	anywayz, rob'll be long gone before things get that far. especially if angela's been feeding him the same hoo-ha she's been feeding us.
zoegirl:	i guess
zoegirl:	it kind of startles me that she'd even consider the possibility.
mad maddie:	u don't think about it? ever?
mad maddie:	oh, wait, ur saint zoe. of course u don't.
zoegirl:	of course i THINK about it, but that's all.
mad maddie:	well, that's all angela's doing. she *thought* about it with dixon schaeffer too, remember? and that scott guy from the pool?
zoegirl:	oh yeah.
zoegirl:	pulling onto your street. see you soon!

Sat, Sept 18, 6:00 PM E.D.T.

SnowAngel:	omg, this sucks.
mad maddie:	what sucks?
SnowAngel:	me, my life, MY MOM.
SnowAngel:	maddie, it's saturday night and i'm stuck at home with chrissy, who discovered "grey's anatomy" on netflix and is now watching every single episode of every single season. this SUPER sucks.
SnowAngel:	(altho, fine. still a good show, at least in the beginning. and patrick dempsey still hot hot hot.)
mad maddie:	oh, that's right. yr grounded. zoe called, but she didn't give me the full story.
SnowAngel:	i shld have known something was wrong when my mom picked me up from your house yesterday. she

	was all "hello, angela" in this frosty, ice-queen way, but i didn't care cuz rob and i were SUPPOSED to go to a movie tonight and i was imagining the romantic possibilities of snuggling in the theater together.
SnowAngel:	but then my mom axed all of that, thx very much.
mad maddie:	**sorry, babe**
SnowAngel:	aaargh! the whole thing is SO not a big deal, but she's making it out to be a federal case. she waited till we were halfway home and then she said, "angela, i read a note in your french book, and i know u didn't go to the library thursday night."
mad maddie:	**well, no, cuz u were at the dark horse**
SnowAngel:	she was like, "how can i trust u? ur the only member of the family who is dishonest, angela, and i consider this a character flaw."
mad maddie:	**a character flaw—yowza. the moms hasn't laid that one on me yet.**
SnowAngel:	i just kinda plummeted inside myself, the way i always do when i'm confronted with something "wrong" that i've done.
SnowAngel:	thank god she didn't realize it was a bar i'd gone to—then i'd really be dead. she just thinks i met up with rob and hung out, but apparently that's bad enough, cuz now i'm stuck at home with my 12-year-old sister while george o'malley holds his finger over a hole in some dude's heart.
mad maddie:	**aw, george. i remember george!**
SnowAngel:	he's pretty adorakable. u shld bike over and watch it with us! please, please, please!!! 🚲
mad maddie:	**can't, sorry. i'm already biking to work. i pulled over when i heard yr special angela txt tone, cuz i'm just that awesome.**
SnowAngel:	yeah, yeah. zoe's out with her parents, ur off to

serve beignets with that cute waiter guy, and here
i'll be, drowning myself in an endless pool of misery.

mad maddie:	**it could be worse.**
SnowAngel:	how?
mad maddie:	**chrissy cld be watching a "shake it up" marathon.**
SnowAngel:	omg. true!!!
SnowAngel:	but still, it's just wrong. i was like, "ok, mom, fine. i've learned my lesson. now can i plz go out?" i totally begged her, and she still said no.
SnowAngel:	she is ruining my life!
mad maddie:	**damn her oily hide**
SnowAngel:	i'm serious!
mad maddie:	**i know, but i've gotta hit the road, yo. we still doing our math together tomorrow?**
SnowAngel:	yeah. i'm allowed to do homework with ppl, i just can't go out with rob. i feel so bad for him, cuz now HIS night is totally ruined too!

Sat, Sept 18, 6:23 PM E.D.T.

mad maddie:	**me again**
SnowAngel:	did u change yr mind? r u coming over?!!
mad maddie:	**i am at work! some of us have to work. must we go over this again?**
mad maddie:	**i just wanted to ask—did u notice that zoe didn't mention friday morning fellowship at all yesterday? not during the school day, not after school, and not at my house last night?**
SnowAngel:	well, duh. cuz she knew u'd make fun of her.
mad maddie:	**and get damned to hell? heavens, no.**
mad maddie:	**did she tell *you* anything about it? is she going back next friday?**
SnowAngel:	*sigh* must we talk about this now?
SnowAngel:	i'm really too depressed.

mad maddie:	**spill**
SnowAngel:	she said the drive with mr. h was really good. they had this great talk about relativism (???) and what a cop-out it is, or something like that, so i think she's going back, yes.
mad maddie:	**blah**
SnowAngel:	*shrugs*
SnowAngel:	it's her life. at least she *has* one!

Mon, Sept 20, 4:45 PM E.D.T.

SnowAngel:	zooooeeeeeee! *stomp stomp stomp*
zoegirl:	angelaaaaaa! why the stomping?
SnowAngel:	cuz i'm pissed!!!!! 😡
zoegirl:	why?
SnowAngel:	BECAUSE! cuz stupid rob went out anyway, and he didn't even tell me!
zoegirl:	angela, what r u talking about?
SnowAngel:	i was heading out after school, and tonnie wyndham came twiddling over and said, "i hear ur going out with rob. that's great!" only she didn't say it like it was great. she said it in this fake-surprised way, like rob's dating down or something cuz i'm not a cheerleader.
zoegirl:	tonnie is not the best person to trust when it comes to character judgments. you know that.
SnowAngel:	i said, "yeah, we've only been dating for a week, but it seems like so much longer. we have the most amazing connection." and tonnie was like, "i know. that's why it was so sad that u couldn't come with us saturday night."
SnowAngel:	i said, "huh?" and she goes, "me and rob and tim and eric. didn't rob tell u?"
zoegirl:	rob went out with tonnie? while you were grounded?
SnowAngel:	well, they didn't GO OUT go out.

SnowAngel:	they just hung together at eric's house.
zoegirl:	still!
SnowAngel:	it gets worse. cuz then rob strolls up, and i said, "sounds like u had a good time saturday night. u could have called me, u know." and tonnie jumped in and said, "he wanted to, but i told him not to."
SnowAngel:	i said, "oh yeah, sure," and rob said, "really, angie. i was just about to hit 'call,' but tonnie said it wld just bum u out to know that we were having such a blast without u."
zoegirl:	!!! what did tonnie say?
SnowAngel:	she didn't say anything. she just stood there pretending to be all sympathetic, nodding away like one of those bobblehead dogs.
zoegirl:	what did you say to rob?
SnowAngel:	i said, "hey, no problem," but the whole thing makes me so mad!
SnowAngel:	i can't stand it that rob was going to call me and tonnie told him not to. SHE IS NOT THE BOSS OF HIM!
zoegirl:	yuck, yuck, yuck. why didn't he just call anyway?
SnowAngel:	cuz he's nice. cuz he was trying to do the right thing, and he probably thought it *wld* bum me out. which it wld have, but it still wld have been better than nothing.
SnowAngel:	ANYWAY, i told him to call me when he got home. it better be soon!

Tues, Sept 21, 5:34 PM E.D.T.

mad maddie:	**zo-ster!**
zoegirl:	madster!
mad maddie:	**i just got home from some excellent driving practice with good ol' moms and found a long-ass voicemail from angela, only now she's not answering her phone. what's up with that?**

zoegirl:	she went shopping with chrissy. i guess her mom didn't consider that part of being grounded?
zoegirl:	but her phone's probably buried in her purse or something.
mad maddie:	**is she still being a pouty-pants about rob?**
zoegirl:	pretty much. she saw him talking to tonnie in the hall today.
mad maddie:	**ooo—talking in the hall. tsk, tsk.**
zoegirl:	i know. she's kind of overreacting.
mad maddie:	**she's moved straight from her starry-eyed phase into her wounded-lover stage. which is good, if for no other reason than she's at least cut back with the devirginization business.**
zoegirl:	there is that
mad maddie:	**did she tell u what happened in math?**
zoegirl:	does it have to do with devirginization?
mad maddie:	**no, it has to do with her being all mopey cuz she's NOT gonna be devirginized.**
mad maddie:	**and before i explain, u've got to understand that usually in math class angela IS THE BIGGEST CHATTERBOX EVER.**
zoegirl:	no!
mad maddie:	**yes! mr. miklos is CONSTANTLY trying to make her shut up. well, today, mr. miklos said to the whole class, "what test do u want on friday, a 1, 2, or 3?"**
zoegirl:	huh?
mad maddie:	**oh yeah, ur in smart math so u dunno about this.**
mad maddie:	**in dumb math, whenever we have a test, it can either be a series 1, 2, or 3, with 3 being the hardest. not that a 3 would be hard for U, but for us dummies, it can be quite traumatic.**
zoegirl:	maddie? shut up and finish the story.
mad maddie:	**so mr. miklos asked that about the test, and when**

	no one answered, he said, "in that case, shld i choose, or shld we play a game of chance?"
mad maddie:	we certainly didn't want the devil choosing, so we took the game of chance. he put three marbles in a bag and said that if he pulled out a red marble, we'd have a 1, if he pulled out a blue one, we'd have a 2, and if he pulled out a white one, we'd have a 3.
mad maddie:	first he pulled out a blue one, and we all yelled, "no fair! rigged! rigged!"
zoegirl:	you have a strange math class.
mad maddie:	so he tried again and pulled out a white one, which meant the HARDEST test, and this time everyone said, "cheater pants! do-over, do-over!"
mad maddie:	he was half frustrated but half having fun, so i offered a brilliant solution. i said, "hey, mr. miklos, how about if angela doesn't say a word for the entire class. THEN will u give us a series 1?"
zoegirl:	did he go for it?
mad maddie:	HA! mr. miklos thought there was no way angela could do it, but angela sat there glum and depressed for the WHOLE CLASS! it was awesome!
zoegirl:	did angela think it was awesome?
mad maddie:	i teased her about it afterward, and she got all grunty and spouted off.
mad maddie:	but, hey—if she's going to be depressed, we might as well get something good out of it.
zoegirl:	like i said: a verrrrry strange math class.
zoegirl:	so how'd the driving go? all set for your license?
mad maddie:	don't u know it. today i drove on northside parkway for the very first time. there were SO MANY CARS BEHIND ME, and i was like, "ahhh! pressure!"

mad maddie: the moms screamed, "slow down! slow down!" and her foot kept pumping away at her own pretend brake on her side of the car. it didn't work, tho. her pretend brake.

zoegirl: because it was pretend?

mad maddie: bingo!

mad maddie: hey, i'm forwarding u and angela a quiz called "what pattern r u?" go take it and then come back and tell me what u r.

zoegirl: i'm supposed to tell you what *pattern* i am? um, what pattern are you?

mad maddie: i am LEOPARD PRINT, baby. rebellious, independent, and unique. and here's ten zillion diamond points saying yr going to be tan, or beige, or . . . i dunno. burnt umber.

zoegirl: those aren't patterns. those are colors.

mad maddie: take the quiz: <u>quizilla.teennick.com/ quizzes/23851466/what-pattern-are-you</u>!

Tues, Sept 21, 5:58 PM E.D.T.

zoegirl: i'm STRIPES! refined, classic, and modest.

mad maddie: stripes, eh? i can see that. beautiful beige and tan stripes.

zoegirl: yeah, and i can see you as leopard print—when you're not wearing jeans and your shit-stomping boots, that is.

mad maddie: i love my shit-stomping boots!

Wed, Sept 22, 9:02 PM E.D.T.

mad maddie: u will not BELIEVE what just happened.

SnowAngel: does it have to do with rob and tonnie? cuz i don't think i can take anymore. she's trying to steal him away from me. i KNOW she is.

mad maddie: god, angela, cld u be more obsessed? no, it

doesn't have to do with rob or tonnie. has to do with jana. i ran into her just now when i was shuttling the moms around, doing my learner's permit escort service of glory.

mad maddie: the moms is in kroger doing some grocery shopping (i.e. getting the pops more beer), so i'm killing time at 7-11. i'm still here, but jana and terri have left.

SnowAngel: did you scare them away?

mad maddie: i wish.

mad maddie: jana and terri were by the magazine stand when i came in. margie walker was there too, altho she wasn't with jana and terri, of course.

SnowAngel: of course

mad maddie: so jana and terri start checking out margie's new do, and jana's all, "god, margie. u have got to stop screwing with your hair!"

SnowAngel: typical. geez, let margie shave her head if that's what she wants to do. what skin is it off jana's nose?

mad maddie: actually, it *was* the tiniest bit funny. i mean, i'm surprised margie has any hair left, the way she's always dyeing it and cutting it and shit. she might end up shaving it for real.

mad maddie: anywayz, margie left with her coffee and a scowl, and i walked past jana and terri to get to the slurpee machine. i gave them a quick nod, but that's all.

SnowAngel: good. she needs to know that not everyone's gonna fawn all over her.

mad maddie: yeah, but then terri left, and it was just me and jana. jana strolled over to the slurpee machine and said, "hey, maddie. what's up?"

SnowAngel: ???

mad maddie: i know! she was . . . normal! and then we had an honest-to-god conversation. it was so weird.

SnowAngel:	what'd u talk about?
mad maddie:	**random stuff, like how she wishes they'd bring sour cherry slurpees back and crap like that. and i was like, "i am so with u. enough of this strawberry-kiwi garbage! bring back the real flavors!"**
SnowAngel:	then she asked if i'd driven to 7-11 myself, meaning did i have my actual driver's license, and i told her no, but that i'd be getting it in october. she was all, "i am soooo jealous. i hate having to depend on my mom for rides, and my bday's not till april."
SnowAngel:	too bad for jana. zoe and i, on the other hand, will have the luverly mads to chauffeur us around IN TWO WEEKS! 😎
mad maddie:	**u got that straight**
SnowAngel:	that's bizarre that jana lowered herself enough to talk to u, huh?
SnowAngel:	u know i'm kidding
mad maddie:	**i'm sure she'll go back to ignoring me at school tomorrow, so don't worry.**
SnowAngel:	why wld i worry? i don't give a damn what jana does.
mad maddie:	**right. me neither.**
mad maddie:	**HEY, did ya take the pattern quiz?**
SnowAngel:	u wld have to ask, wouldn't u? u cldn't just let it go.
SnowAngel:	YES, i took the pattern quiz, and u know what it said i am? TIE-DYE! *pulls hair by roots*
mad maddie:	**what's wrong with tie-dye?**
SnowAngel:	UM, EXCUSE ME.
SnowAngel:	do i wear tevas? noooooooo. do i smell nastily of patchouli? nooooooo. do i write all my english papers on the legalization of marijuana? noooooooo and noooooooooo again!!!!!
mad maddie:	**u liked what the quiz had to say, then. u agreed with its assessment.** 👍

SnowAngel: please. tie-dye is SOOOOOOO last . . . what's the
                 word for lots and lots of decades ago?

mad maddie: pelt-woman wears tie-dye all the time.

SnowAngel: pelt-woman?

mad maddie: mark's girlfriend, remember?

SnowAngel: ur comparing me to the chick who doesn't shave
                 her pubes. lovely.

mad maddie: i'll bring u a hemp necklace tomorrow.

SnowAngel: NOT funny!!!

                 Thu, Sept 23, 3:01 PM E.D.T.

SnowAngel: zoe, what is wrong with the world?! *wails and
                 gnashes teeth*

SnowAngel: rob asked tonnie wyndham to go to carl's party with
                 me and him on friday!!!

zoegirl: what?! i was JUST talking to u and rob. when did
                 this happen?

SnowAngel: just now. i haven't even left the hall. my legs won't
                 work.

zoegirl: your legs will work, angela. tell me what happened.

SnowAngel: ok, so u left, and i was getting my books together,
                 and rob was keeping me company cuz he is just
                 that sweet.

SnowAngel: and then! out of nowhere! tonnie flounced up and
                 starts telling rob how he was soooooooooo funny
                 during english and how it was sooooooooo great that
                 he got mr. kirk to give everyone an extension on
                 their papers.

SnowAngel: i was like, "go away, tonnie! u r soooooooo
                 annoying and that t-shirt is soooooooooo ugly!" it was
                 super super tight and had the word "trouble" written
                 across it in sequins. *gag*

zoegirl: did you really say that to her, that she was
                 annoying?

SnowAngel:	no, but i wanted to.
SnowAngel:	so tonnie says, "what r u two lovebirds up to this weekend?" and very sweetly i grabbed rob's hand and said, "nothing much, just hanging out."
SnowAngel:	rob goes, "what about carl's party? aren't we going to carl's party?" and tonnie squeals, "carl balkin? r his parents going out of town?"
SnowAngel:	and then, out of utter cluelessness, rob goes, "yeah, u should come, right, angela?"
zoegirl:	ick! 😷
zoegirl:	what did you say???
SnowAngel:	i said, "oh, i wish u could, but it's only for ppl who don't wear sequins. sorry!"
zoegirl:	REALLY?
SnowAngel:	no.
SnowAngel:	so now tonnie's coming with us to carl's tomorrow night. we're even picking her up! *bangs head on locker*
zoegirl:	is she honestly hitting on rob, or is she just being . . . i don't know . . . friendly?
SnowAngel:	do u even have to ask? as soon as tonnie walked off, i said to rob, all jokey, "guess u've got a date with 2 girls now. ooo—menage a trois!" he laughed, but he shot me this look like he was kinda nervous.
SnowAngel:	BUT HERE IS THE POINT OF EXTREME IMPORTANT-NESS:
SnowAngel:	if tonnie's coming to carl's then u and maddie have to come 2, cuz i'll need u for moral support. ok?
zoegirl:	angela . . .
SnowAngel:	what?
zoegirl:	i hate those kinds of parties, you know that. where everyone gets trashed and i feel like a loser because i don't drink.
SnowAngel:	u have to come. plz? u can just hold a beer and take little sips every so often.

zoegirl:	i don't want to take little sips every so often. i hate beer.
SnowAngel:	then i'll pour a sprite in a cup for u and we'll tell everyone it's a wine cooler. no one cares!!!
zoegirl:	i don't know. my mom would kill me.
zoegirl:	have you already asked maddie?
SnowAngel:	not yet, but i'm sure she'll come. please, please, please, please, please? u can spy on tonnie and rob for me!
zoegirl:	grrrrrrrr
SnowAngel:	PLEASE??? yr support in this time of need *might* just make it so that my legs work again so that i can leave this stinkin hallway!
zoegirl:	fine, all right. but i'll have to tell my mom we're doing homework together and see if she can give me a ride to your house. and maybe i just won't mention the party at all.
SnowAngel:	*SUPERFLYINGTACKLEPOUNCE!* yay! it's gonna be so much fun—we can make snide remarks to each other and roll our eyes whenever tonnie says anything!!!
zoegirl:	wh-hoo!
SnowAngel:	OH! and speaking of parties, we have GOT to plan maddie's surprise party. her bday's two weeks from tomorrow!
zoegirl:	yikes, you're right
SnowAngel:	i think we should have it at collier park. everybody can bring food and we'll have a twilight picnic.
zoegirl:	who should we invite besides megan and kristin and mary kate?
SnowAngel:	tonnie? *throws head back and laffs maniacally* jana whitaker? *collapses in a heap of amusement*
zoegirl:	having fun?
SnowAngel:	oh, i crack myself up.

zoegirl:	did you see jana and maddie in the cafeteria line, though? they were chatting away like it was perfectly normal.
SnowAngel:	yeah, that was creepy. later i said, "maddie? is there something u want to tell me?" and she goes, "jana's not as bad as i thought she was. she's actually kinda funny."
zoegirl:	OMIGOSH SHE'S BEEN TAKEN OVER BY AN EVIL SPIRIT
SnowAngel:	i know!
SnowAngel:	i was kidding when i said we should invite her (obviously), but let's start telling ppl tomorrow.
zoegirl:	okay. only don't worry if i'm not at school right on time, because i might be a little late.
SnowAngel:	cuz of friday morning fellowship?
zoegirl:	last week we didn't get back until the beginning of first period
SnowAngel:	what did ms. andrist say?
zoegirl:	she didn't care.
SnowAngel:	hmmph. she would if it were a coven meeting.
SnowAngel:	did u hear that announcement about the shakespeare festival? "this year we will not accept any booths concerning witchcraft or fortune-telling unless they specifically pertain to shakespeare's plays."
zoegirl:	bummer. do u care?
SnowAngel:	no
zoegirl:	all right then. and how about your legs? do they work again?
SnowAngel:	*wiggles legs experimentally* hey hey! i can walk! i can WALK! I CAN WALK!!!!

Thu, Sept 23, 11:15 PM E.D.T.

mad maddie: hello, zo. i am txting u out of boredom even tho

	i know yr asleep. why do u go to bed so frickin early, fool?
zoegirl:	i don't ALWAYS. i'm finishing some research for my english paper, thank you very much.
mad maddie:	ooo, for mr. h? kissy, kissy.
zoegirl:	shut up
mad maddie:	ur not going to that fellowship thing again tomorrow, r u?
zoegirl:	i am, and please don't make fun of me.
mad maddie:	well . . . since you asked so nicely. but can we make fun of angela and this dumb party she's dragging us to?
zoegirl:	absolutely
mad maddie:	she needs to lighten up about this whole rob and tonnie deal. if there IS something going on b/w rob and tonnie, then angela should drop rob on his ass and be done with it. and if there ISN'T, then rob should drop angela on hers, cuz i'm sure she's driving him just as nuts as she's driving us.
zoegirl:	you don't think tonnie's t-r-o-u-b-l-e?
mad maddie:	HA! she bitched about that to u too! when u KNOW she would totally wear that shirt herself if she'd found it first.
zoegirl:	that thought did cross my mind . . .
mad maddie:	ah, well. so we'll go to this party at carl's and it'll be dorky, but that's ok cuz we'll be together.
zoegirl:	yeah, but don't say anything to my mom about it. (not that u would.) hey, i've got to finish this essay, k?
mad maddie:	sure, sure. such a good girl you are.
mad maddie:	i'm a good girl too, tho. wanna know why?
zoegirl:	why?
mad maddie:	cuz i changed my very own sheets this afternoon. aren't i so virtuous?

zoegirl: you are the queen of virtue, yes.

mad maddie: it'd been over two months. they were starting to reek!

Fri, Sept 24, 7:29 PM E.D.T.

SnowAngel: maddie, i sure hope yr getting dolled up for the party. r u getting dolled up for the party?

mad maddie: angela, u promised u weren't gonna get all freaky about this. i don't do "dolled up," remember?

SnowAngel: yeah, but zoe's already here and rob's gonna be here any minute, and then we're coming to pick up u and stupid tonnie. 😐 i just want everything to go well.

mad maddie: lighten up—it's just a party.

mad maddie: what r u wearing? i know how u love to discuss these things, and i'm pretty sure that's the real reason u txted. so go on. lay it on me.

SnowAngel: well . . . *since* you asked. attire: swirly dragon t-shirt, white jeans (i read recently that guys LOVE girls in white jeans), sapphire ring, my red heels from zappos. scent: vanilla musk.

mad maddie: fab

SnowAngel: and u?

mad maddie: gray sweats and the pops' wifebeater shirt

SnowAngel: maddie!

mad maddie: jk

SnowAngel: eeek—rob's here! he just pulled in the drive. SEE U SOON!!!

Sat, Sept 25, 10:43 AM E.D.T.

mad maddie: some party last night, hmm?

zoegirl: ack. and that's i why i HATE parties. why does angela never believe me when i tell her i hate parties?!!!

mad maddie: i know what u mean. i always feel awkward, like i don't belong.

zoegirl: yeah, right, miss thang. i saw you shaking your booty to all the dance songs.

mad maddie: for your information, i was dancing ironically.

zoegirl: you were a dancing fool

mad maddie: whatevs. it's cuz i had a couple of beers.

zoegirl: uh . . . yeah. everybody had a couple of beers except for me, even kristin and megan who last year didn't drink at all.

zoegirl: and then everyone looked at me like "ooo, geek girl," like i was going to report them to the honor council.

mad maddie: so just have a beer, for crying out loud!

zoegirl: no thanks

mad maddie: is it cuz of christ our lord? cuz he drank the wine, zo.

zoegirl: i'm not going to drink just because other people do, thank you very much. it's stupid.

zoegirl: mr. h told me that he used to be a total hellion, that he'd drive around with his buddies and bash in trash cans and stuff. but then he realized he was just doing it to be cool, so he stopped.

zoegirl: he says it takes strength to be true to yourself.

mad maddie: mr. h claimed to be a *hellion*?

zoegirl: well, yeah. so?

mad maddie: and he used that very word? "hellion"?? it's like he's trying to be all badass to impress u.

zoegirl: he also told me how he used to only listen to metal bands, but he doesn't anymore, now that he's a christian.

mad maddie: this just gets better and better. does he tell everyone this stuff, or just u?

zoegirl:	he's NICE, maddie. he listens to me. he cares what i have to say.
zoegirl:	and i might as well tell you, i think i'm going to go to church with him tomorrow.
mad maddie:	**wtf?!!**
zoegirl:	well, ok, i AM going to church with him tomorrow.
mad maddie:	**WTF?!!!!!**
zoegirl:	he invited me on the way to fellowship on friday. it sounds cool.
zoegirl:	there's nothing wrong with trying it out.
mad maddie:	**zoe, are angela and i gonna have to hire a deprogrammer to come rescue u from some cabin? r u gonna become mr. h's love slave?**
zoegirl:	you're so overreacting. it's a CHURCH, maddie.
mad maddie:	**how r u gonna get there? oh god, is he picking u up? is this a DATE?**
zoegirl:	maddie . . .
mad maddie:	**what does your mom say about all this?**
zoegirl:	she thinks it's fine. she thinks it's good that i'm broadening my horizons.
mad maddie:	**one way to put it . . .**
mad maddie:	**so IS he picking u up? u avoided the question.**
zoegirl:	yes, maddie, he's picking me up. but it's NO. BIG. DEAL.
mad maddie:	**uh huh. *extremely* fishy.**
zoegirl:	i knew you were going to act like this. i totally knew it. i thought, because you are my FRIEND, that i should include you in my life, but your attitude is really bugging me.
mad maddie:	**well, sorreee**
zoegirl:	i've got to go. i've got a ton of homework.
mad maddie:	**but . . . but . . . we didn't get to gossip about rob and angela!**

zoegirl:	drat. oh well.
mad maddie:	did i tell u i saw rob grab tonnie's ass on the way to the keg?
zoegirl:	u DID?
mad maddie:	well, not exactly, but he laughed at her stupid jokes all night. i hate "dumb blond" jokes, and i'm not even blond.
zoegirl:	yes u are
mad maddie:	i'm dirty blond. doesn't count!

Sun, Sept 26, 11:32 AM E.D.T.

mad maddie:	lovely morning, isn't it? the birds r singing, the sun is shining, the bald man from across the street has shut off his cursed lawn mower ...
SnowAngel:	what makes u so chipper today?
mad maddie:	moi? nothing, other than the fact that i had a great time at work last night. speaking of, what happened to u and rob? i thought u two were gonna come by and have an order of huey's delicious beignets.
SnowAngel:	i thought so too, but all rob wanted to do was hang out in his basement and play pool. said he was still hungover from carl's party.
mad maddie:	oh. that sounds fun. i guess.
SnowAngel:	it was boring.
SnowAngel:	what happened at huey's?
mad maddie:	the kitchen guy, sam, found a roach under one of the counters, a really, really big one with long, waving antennas.
SnowAngel:	ewwwwww!
mad maddie:	it gets better. r u ready?
SnowAngel:	no
mad maddie:	he microwaved it.
SnowAngel:	maddie!!! EWWWWW!!!!

mad maddie: and then phil, the manager, came back and saw what was going on, cuz all the kitchen guys were cheering and making a lot of noise. he fired sam on the spot.

SnowAngel: and this is why u had such a great time at work? a roach got murdered and the kitchen guy was fired?

mad maddie: nooooooo, just be patient. remember that cute waiter ur always going on about?

SnowAngel: *perks up* the shy one with the adorable dimples?

mad maddie: well, his name's ian. he and i were standing over to the side while all this was going on, and we kept giving each other looks, like, "do u believe this?" and once he leaned close to say something, and his arm brushed mine.

SnowAngel: ah-HA!

mad maddie: and after work we sat outside and listened to an awesome playlist he'd made of old-time blues masters, like sonny boy williamson.

SnowAngel: omg!!! *dance, dance*

mad maddie: calm down. he knows i like music, that's all.

SnowAngel: yeah right, that's all. go, mads!!!

Mon, Sept 27, 7:19 PM E.D.T.

SnowAngel: so i didn't see u after 6th period and i have to know: was it weird seeing mr. h in class, after going to church with him and everything?

zoegirl: it kind of was, actually. not bad-weird, just . . . weird, because i feel like i know him as so much more than a teacher, u know?

SnowAngel: like how?

zoegirl: going to church with him AT ALL, first of all. you don't usually go to church with one of your teachers, right?

zoegirl: and then we just had such good conversations on

the way to and from alpharetta, where his church is. it was a long drive, so we got to talk A LOT. he's so interesting, angela, and he knows so much about spirituality. i know maddie makes fun of him, but i really admire him.

SnowAngel: do u think HE thought it was weird today?

zoegirl: i don't know. i may have been making it up. in fact, i probably was. but sometimes it seemed like he was giving me these looks, like he and i shared a secret.

zoegirl: or not a *secret*, more like just the knowledge of the special time we had together.

zoegirl: agh, that sounds corny.

SnowAngel: huh

SnowAngel: zo, don't get offended . . . but do u think he's hitting on u? just a little?

zoegirl: PLEASE

zoegirl: anyway, he told me that he doesn't believe in dating just for the sake of dating. he only wants to date someone if he thinks she might be a person he'd like to marry.

SnowAngel: what if yr that person?

zoegirl: i'm 15, angela.

SnowAngel: so?

zoegirl: although something happened that was sort of funny. when he dropped me off after church, he reached over to open my door for me, and it was a little awkward because his body was, like, right there. soooo close. and then he half-laughed and started to say something, but he stopped himself.

zoegirl: i said, "what?" and he said, "i'll, ah, tell you when you're older."

SnowAngel: zoe!!!!!

zoegirl: DON'T tell maddie.

SnowAngel:	i won't 😵
SnowAngel:	but do u like him? as in, like him like him?
zoegirl:	he's my teacher, angela.
SnowAngel:	how old do u think he is, anyway?
zoegirl:	he's 24. he told me.
SnowAngel:	that's not that much older than u. that's only 9 years. my dad is 11 years older than my mom. *waggles eyebrows*
zoegirl:	well, it doesn't matter because he's my teacher. time to change the subject.
SnowAngel:	wow. u and mr. h.
zoegirl:	angela!
SnowAngel:	ok, ok. so u wanna hear something sad? chrissy got home from school today and said—to me—"my friend lena thinks ur cute, but not pretty."
SnowAngel:	nice, huh? oh, and that chrissy, on the other hand, was pretty as well as cute. as in, prettier than me. BLAH!
zoegirl:	oh, angela. what does lena know, whoever she is?
SnowAngel:	i know, but still. "cute but not pretty"?
SnowAngel:	and then chrissy saw that she'd hurt my feelings, and she tried to apologize by telling me she loved me. the whole thing was pathetic.
zoegirl:	angela? this lena chick is in 7th grade. she knows NOTHING.
SnowAngel:	u know what the worst part was? how ashamed i felt, in this embarrassed, low-down way.
zoegirl:	no! stop! you have *nothing* to feel ashamed of! first of all, you're gorgeous—you know you're the prettiest of you, me, and maddie—and second of all, it doesn't matter what anybody says.
SnowAngel:	do you think chrissy's prettier than i am?
SnowAngel:	ugh, i can't believe i'm even asking this. *sticks head in toilet bowl out of pathetic-ness*

zoegirl:	chrissy's a kid, angela. she's got purple braces.
SnowAngel:	my mom thinks chrissy's prettier. i know cuz one time i said it out loud, like, "i know chrissy's prettier than me, but that's ok," and mom didn't contradict me. she said we all have our special qualities.
zoegirl:	angela . . .
SnowAngel:	and to top everything off, rob is being a total penis-head. the only time i got to see him was before french, and he talked to matthew curtis the whole time, which pissed me off.
SnowAngel:	but then i started thinking that it was just as much my fault that we didn't talk, so i called after school to see if i cld go to his house and hang out, thinking maybe that would make everything fun again.
zoegirl:	and?
SnowAngel:	he had some friends over, so he said he'd call me back.
zoegirl:	and??
SnowAngel:	eventually he did. and we talked for a while, and i thought it was going well. *i* thought i was being interesting, even tho he wasn't really responding.
SnowAngel:	then i finished telling him about a dream i'd had and there was absolute silence.
zoegirl:	oh no
SnowAngel:	then, really abruptly, he goes, "well, i'll see u tomorrow, ok?" just out of the blue. it was seriously pretty rude.
zoegirl:	i agree—and strange too.
SnowAngel:	i know! he didn't say, "listen, angela, i've gotta go," or anything like that. he just went, "i'll c u tomorrow," smack in the middle of the conversation.
zoegirl:	he's a jerk
SnowAngel:	except he's NOT, zoe!
SnowAngel:	maybe it's not healthy to like someone as much as

i like him, but i can't help it. when things are good b/w us, they're so so good. he's, like, my soul mate, i swear to god.

zoegirl: i hate to point this out, but you've only been going out with him for a week and a half.

SnowAngel: two weeks exactly. today is our anniversary.

zoegirl: angela . . .

SnowAngel: i know, i know. but i think i've secretly been liking him for a lot longer, and that makes it so much more real.

zoegirl: are you sure he's worth it?

SnowAngel: yes, i'm sure! i'm totally sure! except when he's being an asshole. *grinds teeth*

zoegirl: i think you should let HIM come to YOU next time. make sure he knows that you're not just automatically available 24-7.

SnowAngel: good point.

SnowAngel: okay, i'm not gonna bother with him anymore until he shows a sign of wanting to be bothered.

zoegirl: 👍

zoegirl: anyway, we have maddie's bday party to focus on. i talked to delia in homeroom, and she's totally up for it. that means everyone we invited is coming except mary kate.

SnowAngel: we still need to work out food deets, tho. i wish it was this weekend instead of next.

zoegirl: angela? stop thinking about rob.

SnowAngel: i'll try 😢

Tues, Sept 28, 10:15 PM E.D.T.

mad maddie: did u have a better day today, even tho mr. miklos picked on u in math?

SnowAngel: i guess

SnowAngel: things improved with rob, anyway.

mad maddie: meaning?

SnowAngel:	meaning he apologized for getting off the phone with me so quickly yesterday.
mad maddie:	**good**
SnowAngel:	yeah. i acted all puzzled, like i didn't even know what he was talking about. then u know what i told him?
mad maddie:	**what?**
SnowAngel:	that i'd gone out and walked on the train tracks until midnight, just by myself.
mad maddie:	**u went to the train tracks? by yrself?**
SnowAngel:	hell no! r u crazy?
mad maddie:	**shit, ur always going on about how freaky they r, how ur afraid a hobo is gonna come and molest u.**
SnowAngel:	cuz one cld. u never know.
mad maddie:	**so why'd u say that then? to rob?**
SnowAngel:	cuz i liked the idea of it. cuz i liked the idea of him thinking that i went out and walked all night on the train tracks. it's a lot better than what i really did, which was lie on my bed and listen to Mumford & Sons and feel sorry for myself.
SnowAngel:	but u know what's strange?
mad maddie:	**what?**
SnowAngel:	it made me start wondering how much of other ppl r just images they made up. like maybe ppl lie about all kinds of things—how would we ever know?
mad maddie:	**totally. like today in math, when carl balkin was sitting in the back guffawing with his buds about all the "action" he got with some freshman chick. i was like, "yeah, right, carl. not even a freshman wld get it on with u."**
SnowAngel:	so true
mad maddie:	**and that necklace he was wearing, with all the little metal balls? tray fruitay.**
SnowAngel:	god, i know
SnowAngel:	but u shouldn't use that expression.

mad maddie:	**what expression?**
SnowAngel:	"tray fruitay." it's not nice.
mad maddie:	**???**
mad maddie:	**jana said it this morning in homeroom, and it cracked me up.**
SnowAngel:	yeah, but it's like making fun of someone for being gay.
mad maddie:	**no it's not, cuz it's an insult u could only use on someone who's *not* gay.**
mad maddie:	**if someone was trying to look gay on purpose then it would be no big deal. but if someone looks like an idiot just cuz he is an idiot, then it's his fault and he should be mocked.**
SnowAngel:	but ur mocking him by calling him gay, which is mean to ppl who r gay.
mad maddie:	**oh, plz**
SnowAngel:	u know i'm right
mad maddie:	**don't u think it's the slightest bit funny? tray fruitay?**
SnowAngel:	i think it's funny that U think it's funny, given that it's an expression that came from jana.
mad maddie:	**ohhhhhhh. so it's wrong to use "gay" as an insult, but u can dismiss something just cuz a certain person said it? that's allowed, then?**
SnowAngel:	excuse me?
mad maddie:	**i think ur being hypocritical, that's all.**
SnowAngel:	*steps a safe distance away* o-k-a-a-a-y . . .
mad maddie:	**just drop it.**
SnowAngel:	fine
mad maddie:	**fine**

	Tues, Sept 28, 10:44 PM E.D.T.
mad maddie:	**aargh! i am so annoyed at angela!!!** 😠
zoegirl:	why? what'd she do?

mad maddie: oh, nvm. it's stupid. anyway, i was GOING to give her the personality quiz of the week, but i didn't, so i'm gonna give it to u instead.

zoegirl: lay it on me

mad maddie: it's called "Discover Ur Inner Dragon." wanna hear what it said about me?

zoegirl: sure

mad maddie: As the mighty Blades of old, your Dragon color is . . . COPPER. Coppers show up when someone's about to die. You like to stomp your enemies, incite rebellions, start the occasional war, and spend lazy hours preening your battle aura. Just in case some puny human thinks they can get the drop on you, you've got a concealed breath weapon—gigantic masses of Fire. Hey, it's the tried-and-true way to cook a cow in 0.75 seconds.

zoegirl: what the . . . ? that is weird, maddie. i don't even know what it's talking about.

mad maddie: it's talking about how tough i am, that's what.

zoegirl: where do you find these things???

mad maddie: it's one of my many talents. r u ready to discover your own inner dragon?

zoegirl: no

mad maddie: quiz is at gotoquiz.com/what_type_of_dragon_ are_you_6. report back!

Tues, Sept 28, 10:59 PM E.D.T.

zoegirl: got my results.

mad maddie: and?

zoegirl: As the Day that cleanses and gives Life, your Dragon color is . . . WHITE. You reach for spirituality and look down upon the world from the highest mountain peaks. If someone ever threatens you, your Inner Dragon would likely tell you to hit and run, or just plain run. But if they really wanted a fight you'd be an impressive opponent, considering you pack a breath weapon combination of Fire and Lightning. Even the nicest dragons can do some serious damage.

mad maddie: **c?! it's u to a T, especially the bit about reaching for spirituality. (if that's what u call flirting with mr. h, anywayz)**

zoegirl: ha ha, very funny

mad maddie: **i'm gonna send the link to angela after all, cuz i have to know what she is. betcha a million her color's pink.**

zoegirl: do dragons come in pink?

mad maddie: **hell, i didn't know they came in white.**

Wed, Sept 29, 7:02 PM E.D.T.

mad maddie: **three warm chocolate chip cookies, courtesy of the pillsbury doughboy. IN. MY. BELLY.**

SnowAngel: mmmm. 🍪

mad maddie: **guess what? ONLY 1 WEEK AND 2 DAYS TILL MY BIRTHDAY!!!**

SnowAngel: wh-hoo! *wild, arm-flailing cheerleader jumps*

mad maddie: **i can't freakin wait. the moms promised to take me to get my license that very afternoon, as soon as school lets out.**

SnowAngel: u scared?

mad maddie: **not about the written part, but i'm jittery about the actual driving part. i know i can do all the stuff, but what if i spaz out with the testing guy there in the car with me?**

SnowAngel: i know. my bday's not for three more months, but i still get sweaty thinking about it. ESPECIALLY parallel parking.

mad maddie: **did i tell u what happened when my brother took his test?**

SnowAngel:	no
mad maddie:	he had to weave the car through these orange cones, and he ran over one with his back tire. the guy who was grading him shook his head and said, "sorry, son. u knock over a cone, ur done."
SnowAngel:	oh no! that's TOTALLY gonna happen to me, i know it!
mad maddie:	but when mark pulled forward, the cone sprang back up. the guy looked at the cone, looked at mark, and said, "all right. keep going."
SnowAngel:	no way! HA!
SnowAngel:	did he end up passing the test?
mad maddie:	barely
SnowAngel:	that's hilarious
mad maddie:	so i figure that even if i'm nervous, if mark could pass it then surely i can too.
SnowAngel:	r yr parents gonna let u start driving right away? on your own, i mean?
mad maddie:	i'll have my license, so they'll have to. it's the law.
mad maddie:	but yeah, they're ok with it cuz then i can be their slave girl and do errands for them and shit. the pops had the gremlin checked over by his mechanic, and everything's looking good.
SnowAngel:	IT IS GONNA BE SO AWESOME!!!! the winsome threesome, styling along in the gremlin. *queenly wave to crowds of fawning admirers*
mad maddie:	u know what i've been thinking?
SnowAngel:	what?
mad maddie:	well, remember my road trip fantasy? i think we shld go for it. like maybe after thanksgiving, over the long weekend. wldn't that rock?
SnowAngel:	for real? YES!!! YES, YES, YES, YES, YES!!!!
mad maddie:	i know our parents r gonna shoot it down, especially zoe's. but if we start working on them now, maybe we can convince them.

SnowAngel: omg. we'll have to really plan it out so they can see
                how mature and responsible we're being.

mad maddie: **yeah, so start thinking of places we could drive
                to, places that would be fun but that wouldn't
                push the rents over the edge. like maybe busch
                gardens?**

SnowAngel: ooo—my cousin went there and said it's a blast.
                and seaworld is near there too, right?

mad maddie: **this whole idea may totally not happen—it
                probably won't—but it's worth a try.**

SnowAngel: or maybe it will, cuz we'll MAKE it happen.

SnowAngel: oh, that would just be so cool. and it'll give us
                something to look forward to so we can last till
                thanksgiving.

mad maddie: **i'll have had my license for two months by then,
                which hopefully will count for something.**

SnowAngel: have u told zoe?

mad maddie: **i will in a sec.**

mad maddie: **but first: did u take the "become one with your
                inner dragon" quiz?**

SnowAngel: oh, that. *rolls eyes*

mad maddie: **and?**

SnowAngel: and my results were completely dumb, only ur
                gonna think they're hysterical.

mad maddie: **tell me. come on, come on, come on.**

SnowAngel: *sighs loudly*

SnowAngel: As the vast forests that protect our planet, your
                dragon color is . . . GREEN. You like to commune with
                nature and lobby governments for alternative fuels and
                conservation. Folks shouldn't get the idea you're a
                hippy pushover though, because your breath weapon
                is a nasty fire/acid combination. Maybe you should
                invest in a hemp shirt reading "Don't knock my smock,
                or I'll clean your clock."

mad maddie:	YES! first tie-dye and now communing with nature! u R a hippy chick!
SnowAngel:	enough
mad maddie:	u and pelt-woman, baby. u should go have a moon ceremony together.
SnowAngel:	do u want me to flame u with my breath weapon?
mad maddie:	hee hee hee. i can just c u in a hemp shirt . . .
SnowAngel:	i am spitting fire at u, maddie! if u feel hot, that is why!!!

Fri, Oct 1, 6:30 PM E.D.T.

SnowAngel:	zoe! *bangs on keys* what is WRONG with the world?!!!
zoegirl:	hmm. i'm guessing maybe u'll tell me?
SnowAngel:	what's wrong is that it's 6:30 on friday night, which means i SHLD be preparing for a romantic evening with my boyfriend. but am i? noooooooooo.
SnowAngel:	he was supposed to call right after school to let me know what the plans were, and now it's three hours l8r and HE HASN'T FREAKIN CALLED *OR* TEXTED!!!
zoegirl:	have u called him?
SnowAngel:	i've left FIVE MESSAGES and a gazillion txts. no response.
zoegirl:	maybe he just forgot
SnowAngel:	if he did, that's even worse. *glares murderously*
SnowAngel:	do u know what happened today? do u? i found rob standing by his locker talking to tonnie. he was asking for her advice on the jacket he was wearing, whether he should zip it or leave it unzipped. can u believe that?!!
zoegirl:	um . . . i'm not sure. i mean, i know it was bad for him to be talking to tonnie, but why do u care about the jacket? did u give it to him or something?

SnowAngel:	NO, i didn't give it to him. i just . . . aargh. the first time we went out he was wearing this cute t-shirt that said "moab" on it, and he asked if i thought it was cool or dumb, since he's never been to moab. at the time i thought it was sweet, the fact that he wanted my opinion. then today i saw him playing the same game with tonnie, and it made me feel sick.
zoegirl:	yuck, angela. why don't u just break up with him?
SnowAngel:	i should. i totally shld.
zoegirl:	so why don't u?
SnowAngel:	i dunno. *sighs*
SnowAngel:	it's complicated.
zoegirl:	???
SnowAngel:	this'll sound weird, but it's like i can't just walk away from him cuz then i'd be this big loser. i mean, he's so amazingly smart and funny and adorable, so when i'm around him, i try really hard to be smart and funny and adorable too.
SnowAngel:	it's like i have to earn his respect, u know?
SnowAngel:	i just . . . i want to mean more to him than i do.
zoegirl:	oh, angela 😟
SnowAngel:	i know
zoegirl:	ur not gonna wait around for him all night, r u? please don't sit at yr house waiting for him.
SnowAngel:	don't worry. mom's taking me and chrissy to bennigan's cuz dad has a late meeting. maybe, if he finally does call, i'll pretend *i* forgot.
zoegirl:	that's the spirit.
SnowAngel:	can we talk about something else? something cheerful?
zoegirl:	sure. like what?
SnowAngel:	our road trip!!! *pumps fist in air and whoops like a redneck*

zoegirl:	oh man. my mom is never going to go for it.
SnowAngel:	but did madigan tell u her new idea, about cumberland island? it's way closer than busch gardens, and once we got there we could take a ferry to the island itself and camp out. it wld just be us and the park rangers, so our parents wouldn't have to worry about us partying or anything.
zoegirl:	yeah, we talked about it in homeroom. jana whitaker was listening in, and she said beach camping is really fun.
SnowAngel:	*jana* said that?
zoegirl:	uh huh. the whole time we were talking, jana was like, "road trip. yeah. that's cool." maddie acted as smooth as ever, but i could tell she was pleased.
SnowAngel:	GOD, that makes me sick.
zoegirl:	why?
SnowAngel:	cuz it's soooo not maddie—or at least it used to not be. these days i'm not so sure.
zoegirl:	what do you mean?
SnowAngel:	i don't even wanna get into it, cuz it's like the more we talk about jana the more power she gets.
SnowAngel:	but today in math, maddie was chatting with eric craver, and i heard her say that once she got her license, she was gonna "cruise the back roads and blast some totally cream music."
zoegirl:	blast some totally cream music???
SnowAngel:	it's her new jana-ism. it's just so wrong how she's gone from hating her to, like, worshipping her.
zoegirl:	"worshipping" may be a little extreme. anyway, maybe jana's changed. maybe she's gotten better.
SnowAngel:	i can't believe u wld say that!!! do u know what jana said to me today? DO u?
SnowAngel:	i was doing my nails during my free, and jana

breezes up and goes, "saw u at carl's party with rob. did you getcha some?"

zoegirl: get you some what?

SnowAngel: what do u think?!

SnowAngel: and then she goes, "or was it tonnie who got lucky?" then she fake-laughed and said, "just kidding. honestly, i think it's so big of you not to care that he flirts with other girls."

zoegirl: oh, that's bad

SnowAngel: do u think she knows something that i don't? do u really think he's flirting with tonnie?

zoegirl: i don't know. i hope not. but i wouldn't worry about anything jana says.

SnowAngel: i know, cuz jana is NOT a nice person.

zoegirl: agreed.

zoegirl: here's what i say: go to bennigan's. try to have fun, and DON'T obsess about rob. he's not worth it.

Fri, Oct 1, 9:45 PM E.D.T.

zoegirl: maddie! you there?

mad maddie: um, yeah . . .

mad maddie: where's the fire?

zoegirl: it's angela. we need to go over and be with her— NOW.

mad maddie: ???

zoegirl: she's been crying to me over the phone for the last hour. she went out to dinner with her mom and chrissy, and while she was there, guess who she ran into?

zoegirl: TONNIE AND ROB. as in, on a date. she said they were snuggled up in a booth sharing an awesome blossom.

mad maddie: christ, that sucks.

mad maddie: what the hell is an awesome blossom?

zoegirl: u know, those fried onion thingies with the dipping sauce. and what's worse? angela and rob shared one on their first date too.

mad maddie: is bennigan's the only restaurant rob goes to???

zoegirl: not the point. angela is devastated, so i told her we'd come over and spend the night. watch movies and eat tons and tons of junk food, that sort of thing.

mad maddie: sounds good. i'll see if mark can give me a ride.

zoegirl: on the phone, angela kept saying, "is it cuz tonnie's prettier than me? IS it?" i feel so bad for her.

mad maddie: did she say anything to rob when she saw him? and did he see her?

zoegirl: he saw her, all right. angela said he stared at her for like ten seconds, and then he turned to tonnie and started talking really animatedly, even though a blush had spread from his neck all the way up his face.

zoegirl: angela grabbed chrissy and her mom and jerked them out the door, and then she burst into tears.

mad maddie: that asshole

zoegirl: and then apparently her mom made some super-supportive comment like, "just let it go, angela. he's obviously the type of boy who only cares about appearances."

mad maddie: good lord

zoegirl: so we should get over there, because she's totally a mess.

mad maddie: gotcha. i'm on it!

Sat, Oct 2, 5:22 PM E.D.T.

mad maddie: hey, poor sad angela. your tweet made me want

	to hug you. r u really at krispy kreme, or was that another "walking the lonely train tracks" fake-out?
SnowAngel:	i really am at KK. I walked here, hoping that getting off my butt wld help, but it didn't. so now i'm expanding my butt with donuts.
SnowAngel:	i hate myself, basically.
mad maddie:	don't hate yourself. hate rob. have u talked to him?
SnowAngel:	no
mad maddie:	well, good. he's not worth it.
SnowAngel:	i TELL myself that, but that's not how it feels.
SnowAngel:	i need u and zoe. ur the only ones who understand. you're coming back tonight, right?
mad maddie:	ouch. that's actually why i texted. i want to—i do—but i can't. i'm scheduled to work, and i can't find anyone to trade shifts with.
SnowAngel:	no! u HAVE to!
mad maddie:	but zoe'll be there. u'll be fine.
mad maddie:	i'll call u tomorrow!

Mon, Oct 4, 5:25 PM E.D.T.

SnowAngel:	hey, mads. hey, zo. i had a totally crappy time at school today, just so u both know. *sniffle, sniffle*
mad maddie:	ah, shit. i'm sorry.
SnowAngel:	i didn't wanna go at all, but mom made me. how unfair is that?
mad maddie:	terribly unfair. those damn parents, always wanting their damn kids to go to school. i say we revolt.
zoegirl:	how was french? did u and rob talk?
SnowAngel:	yes. he said that tonnie was the one who asked him out, and he didn't know how to say "no."
mad maddie:	that is the lamest excuse i think i've ever heard. please tell me u told him to go to hell.

SnowAngel:	i told him it really hurt my feelings.
zoegirl:	good for u
mad maddie:	what?!!! he treated u like dirt, angela. telling him he "really hurt your feelings" isn't gonna do it.
SnowAngel:	he also said that tonnie is just a friend, even if she wants to be more, and that he's sorry if he ruined something good just cuz of her.
zoegirl:	IF he ruined something good?
mad maddie:	he's a dick. and he looks like that weird brother guy on "arrested development."
SnowAngel:	he does not!
mad maddie:	zoe? back me up?
zoegirl:	well, not EXACTLY. but kind of. just a *teeny* bit, if he were way older.
mad maddie:	ok, he's the young version of the weird bro on "arrested development." it's still bad!
SnowAngel:	maybe i'll email him. shld i email him? cuz he acted like things were over b/w us when he was telling me about tonnie, but maybe that's just cuz he's afraid i won't give him a second chance.
mad maddie:	ANGELA. STOP RIGHT NOW.
SnowAngel:	but what if it's true love? i can't walk away from true love!
zoegirl:	do you REALLY think it's true love?
SnowAngel:	it MIGHT be. and i don't wanna be the kind of person who's not willing to put in the work, u know? love takes work. it's not all cake and ice cream.
mad maddie:	all right, i can't deal with this. bye, ladies.
SnowAngel:	maddie?
SnowAngel:	zoe, did maddie really go away?
zoegirl:	looks like it
SnowAngel:	maddie doesn't get it, cuz she's never been in love. but it's better to have lived and loved than never to have loved at all.

zoegirl: i guess

SnowAngel: it's TRUE. and now i'm gonna email rob like i said i
               would, cuz u've made me feel so much better.

zoegirl: i have?

SnowAngel: yeah. thanks for the pep talk, i needed it. ⭐

Mon, Oct 4, 5:59 PM E.D.T.

mad maddie: **zoe, angela is her own worst enemy, you know.**

zoegirl: i love her so much, but i do kind of understand
               what you're saying. but i don't know how to tell
               her that to her face. i don't even know if i want to
               say it to her face.

mad maddie: **i do. i just wanna shake her shoulders and say,
               "GET A CLUE! HE IS A LOSER!!!"**

zoegirl: i know. it's so sad.

mad maddie: **yeah, but it's also just ANNOYING.**

mad maddie: **i didn't wanna mention it in front of angela,
               but can i tell u what a great time i had at work
               saturday night?**

zoegirl: with ian?

mad maddie: **we splashed dishwater at each other—it was
               vair vair flirty and fun. and get this: he asked if i
               wanted to hang out with him next weekend, after
               our shifts r over.**

zoegirl: no way!

mad maddie: **way!**

zoegirl: you said yes, i'm assuming?

mad maddie: **oh, i was very coy as i turned bright red and
               mumbled, "uuh, sure!" i was quite the vixen.** 😊

zoegirl: oh, maddie, you are going to have an awesome
               birthday weekend. you're still going out with me
               and angela on friday, right?

mad maddie: **ack—i totally forgot. actually, the rents have had
               a rare moment of parental affection and wanna**

take me to that brazilian restaurant where u get heaps and heaps of meat. sounds like my kind of place, baby.

zoegirl: this friday? they're taking you to Meat Land this friday?

mad maddie: uh, yes, since that would be my bday . . .

zoegirl: but you said u'd go out with us!

mad maddie: so we'll go out saturday instead, only it'll have to be in the morning since i work that night. ooo— we could do the all-u-can-eat breakfast buffet at shoney's!

zoegirl: yeah, but angela had her heart set on being with you on your exact birthday. i don't mean to make a big deal out of this, but she'll be really disappointed if we don't get together.

mad maddie: that's ridiculous

zoegirl: i know, but still. she'd be really, really disappointed. she's just so fragile right now.

mad maddie: fine. i'll tell the rents to take me out another time, i guess.

zoegirl: excellent idea. maybe THEY can take u to shoney's.

mad maddie: whatevs

mad maddie: welp, time to bounce. mark is gonna take me driving in a minute here, and i must do my limbering-up exercises. rotate the wrists, rotate the neck, practice my patented scan for dogs and small children . . .

zoegirl: have fun. 🚗

mad maddie: only four more days!!!

Mon, Oct 4, 7:45 PM E.D.T.

SnowAngel: i wrote rob that email. i'm not gonna show it to

maddie cuz she'd just be mean, but do u wanna read it?

zoegirl: angela. are you sure rob's really worth it?

SnowAngel: here's what it says:

Dear Rob, I just wanted to say that it's totally cool if you want to hang out with other people. Obviously Tonnie is just a friend, because why would anyone choose her when they could have me? Ha ha, just joking. But anyway, we shouldn't let her come between us, because I think we have something really special. Call me, ok? Love, Angela.

zoegirl: oh. well, that's . . . very nice.

SnowAngel: do u think it's too much that i said "love"? cuz i DO love him. but i don't wanna scare him off, especially when he's already feeling guilty. i don't wanna overwhelm him.

zoegirl: don't take this the wrong way, but are you absolutely positive you want to send it? maybe you should just give it some time.

SnowAngel: what good would that do? anyway, i already DID send it.

SnowAngel: omigod, why? do u think i shouldn't have?!!

zoegirl: i didn't say that

SnowAngel: u think i shouldn't have sent it.

SnowAngel: crap. crap!

SnowAngel: u think i'm a freak, don't u? is HE gonna think i'm a freak? oh no, this is terrible!

zoegirl: hold on, angela. just wait and see. there's nothing more you can do.

SnowAngel: i cld write him again. i could try to be more low-key!

zoegirl: NO, angela. just wait and see.

SnowAngel:	right. ok.
SnowAngel:	but i'm gonna go check my email in case he's already responded

Mon, Oct 4, 10:51 PM E.D.T.

SnowAngel:	he didn't write back.
zoegirl:	oh, angela
SnowAngel:	but maybe he hasn't had time to read it. maybe he's been super-busy.
zoegirl:	maybe so
SnowAngel:	i'll check first thing in the morning and tell u what he says!!!

Tues, Oct 5, 10:01 PM E.D.T.

SnowAngel:	zoe, i need u!
zoegirl:	i'm here, i'm here. what happened?
SnowAngel:	I HATE TONNIE WYNDHAM!!! *clomps about in a flying rage*
zoegirl:	what happened?
SnowAngel:	i called rob—just to talk, cuz he never did email me back last night, and in french he was all weird—and he hemmed and hawed and asked if we could do this later.
zoegirl:	"can we do this later"? that's what he said?
SnowAngel:	he said he was playing Call of Duty. i was kinda hurt, but i was like, "sure, whatever." and then over the phone i heard this voice whining, "ro-o-o-ob, look behind you! don't die!" TONNIE WYNDHAM WAS AT HIS HOUSE!!! THEY WERE PLAYING CALL OF DUTY TOGETHER!!!
zoegirl:	NO. WAY. what a loser.
SnowAngel:	i know! i HATE her!!!
zoegirl:	actually, i meant rob.
SnowAngel:	it's not *his* fault. she probably showed up

	unannounced. he doesn't know how to say no to her, remember?
zoegirl:	angela, can you hear yourself? ROB IS A LOSER!
SnowAngel:	but he's so cute! and i miss him so much!
zoegirl:	yeah, but he's treating you like dirt.
SnowAngel:	he is?
zoegirl:	he IS
SnowAngel:	oh
SnowAngel:	well, then i'm not gonna call him back! i was going to, just to let him apologize, cuz i'm sure he feels really shitty. but he'll just have to call me himself!
zoegirl:	good for you
SnowAngel:	we'll see how he likes that, huh?

Tues, Oct 5, 10:12 PM E.D.T.

zoegirl:	omigosh, i did it. i just told angela what a loser rob is and that she has to get over him!
mad maddie:	ooo, way to be tough. did she listen?
zoegirl:	i don't know. but maybe?
mad maddie:	yay, zoe. WAY TO GO!

Wed, Oct 6, 5:33 PM E.D.T.

SnowAngel:	i've made up my mind: i'm gonna stop letting this rob business tear me up.
mad maddie:	for real?
SnowAngel:	cuz it's just stupid, right? why should i waste my life pining after him when all it's gonna do is make me miserable?
mad maddie:	now you're talking. good girl, angela.
SnowAngel:	so i'm on my way to his house right now, only i just biked up a really steep hill so i stopped to take a break. *pant pant*
SnowAngel:	but i'm five minutes away, and when i'm there, we can finally just talk and get it all out.

mad maddie: ANGELA!!! i thought u meant

mad maddie: nvm. but didn't u already talk and get it all out, that day in french?

SnowAngel: no, cuz that's when he thought we weren't gonna be together anymore, which is ridiculous. i mean talk it out in a good way, so we can work out all our problems.

mad maddie: so ur just gonna show up on his doorstep?

SnowAngel: yeah, cuz then he can't turn me away.

mad maddie: er . . . doesn't that tell u something?

SnowAngel: i've caught my breath. bye!

Wed, Oct 6, 5:47 PM E.D.T.

mad maddie: shake a leg, zo. up and at 'em.

zoegirl: huh?

mad maddie: angela's biking over to rob's. she's almost there, and she said she's gonna make him talk things out once and for all.

zoegirl: oh no

mad maddie: so get your mom to drop u off at angela's house. say u've gotta help her with her math or something.

zoegirl: why? she's already left!

mad maddie: yeah, but we'll be there when she gets back.

zoegirl: ohhhhh

mad maddie: we're the ones who have to pick up the pieces!

Thu, Oct 7, 4:01 PM E.D.T.

zoegirl: you doing any better today? you ran off after sixth period before i could find you.

SnowAngel: too busy crying. go away!

zoegirl: but . . . you answered my text. you can't be THAT busy.

SnowAngel: well, i am. and my thumbs hurt. and also i keep

> hoping rob will text or call or email or SOMETHING, and that he'll tell me it was all a big mistake. that tonnie was talking out of her ass, and that the only reason he didn't tell her to shut up was cuz he's too nice of a guy.

SnowAngel:	pathetic, i know
zoegirl:	i don't think he's going to, angela.
SnowAngel:	i said I KNOW! god!
zoegirl:	all right. it's your life!

Thu, Oct 7, 4:30 PM E.D.T.

mad maddie:	have u checked on angela?
zoegirl:	she's a mess. she didn't want to talk to me.
mad maddie:	she wldn't talk to me, either. i texted her, and she said go away. i called her, and she answered, but she was all pissy.
zoegirl:	it's like she's mad at us for being right.
mad maddie:	i know.
zoegirl:	i think she skipped french too, because she didn't want to deal with seeing rob. and i'm glad we ate lunch in the courtyard, because kristin said he and tonnie were all lovey-dovey during lunch.
mad maddie:	yeah, kristin told me that too. don't they have any respect?
zoegirl:	obviously not
zoegirl:	well, at least now angela knows.
mad maddie:	uh, yeah. i'd say the run-in at rob's house probably did the trick. what did tonnie say when angela confronted them? "u brought it on yourself by being so blind"?
zoegirl:	as if angela should have read the signs and figured it out herself, without rob having to spell it out.

mad maddie:	altho the signs WERE there. i mean, WE knew.
zoegirl:	still, rob is a total wimp. it's basically like he had tonnie break up with angela for him.
mad maddie:	oh well. u win some, u lose some. i just hope angela gets out of her funk before tomorrow, cuz in only 7½ short hours . . .
zoegirl:	u turn 16! wh-hoo!!! 💣

Fri, Oct 8, 4:00 PM E.D.T.

zoegirl:	are you ready for maddie's party?
SnowAngel:	we've got almost an hour before we're supposed to be there, zo.
zoegirl:	i know, but i'm so excited! aren't you?
zoegirl:	megan just called to get directions, and she really thinks maddie has no clue.
SnowAngel:	maybe. i dunno.
zoegirl:	angela! snap out of it. this is MADDIE'S PARTY, remember?
SnowAngel:	i'm just . . . i'm not really in the party mood.
zoegirl:	so get in the party mood. forget rob and forget tonnie. are they really more important than your best friend's party?
SnowAngel:	*flutters fingers lethargically in air*
zoegirl:	are you dressed, at least? what are you going to wear?
SnowAngel:	ur just asking to cheer me up. ur trying to distract me.
zoegirl:	no, i really want to know.
SnowAngel:	*sighs*
SnowAngel:	mermaid print shirt, faded levi's, maddie's bottle-cap belt, brown leather clogs. scent: hard candy.
zoegirl:	that sounds so cute! i bet you look TERRIFIC.
SnowAngel:	oh, and my blue old navy hoodie tied around my waist, in case it gets chilly.

zoegirl:	excellent idea
SnowAngel:	u know, i really DO need this tonight. after my hell week, i mean. i just need to get out and be with u guys.
zoegirl:	i hear you. oh, and check this out. mr. h asked what my plans were this weekend. isn't that odd?
SnowAngel:	he DID?
zoegirl:	after english, after everyone else left the room. it's odd, isn't it?
SnowAngel:	i dunno. a little, maybe.
SnowAngel:	what did u say?
zoegirl:	that we were having a surprise party for maddie. he asked if boys were coming, and i said no. then he got this funny look on his face and said, "good."
SnowAngel:	what does THAT mean?
zoegirl:	that he doesn't want me lured away by some sophomore hottie, because he wants me for himself? JUST KIDDING!!!
SnowAngel:	shit, zoe, i bet that's exactly what it meant.
zoegirl:	i said i was KIDDING.
SnowAngel:	i mean it. he's flirting with u.
zoegirl:	you really think so?
SnowAngel:	omg, u sound pleased.
SnowAngel:	u better be careful, zo. take it from me: ALL GUYS SUCK.
zoegirl:	maybe so. that doesn't mean all MEN do!

Sat, Oct 9, 11:14 AM E.D.T.

mad maddie:	**red-hot! our team is red-hot! our team is R-E-D! H-O-T! and once we start we can't be stopped! goooooooooo team!**
SnowAngel:	maddie? um, what r u talking about?
zoegirl:	i think she's doing a cheer. you know, like a cheerleader would do.

mad maddie: thank u SO MUCH for my surprise party!!!! U R AWESOME!!!!!

zoegirl: you're so welcome! it was fun!!!

SnowAngel: were u really and truly surprised?

mad maddie: i was. it was perfect. and i was so glad that u were back among the living. i was really gonna have to hate u if u were a sourpuss on my big day.

SnowAngel: thx, i guess. last night was great, but this morning i woke up missing rob again. i still am really sad.

mad maddie: i know, i know

mad maddie: but the pops is blaring the horn for me to get my fanny to the car. bday brunch, u know.

SnowAngel: try to have fun. and have fun at work tonight, bday girl!!! 🎂

Sun, Oct 10, 1:12 PM E.D.T.

mad maddie: i hope yr there, cuz i have big news. big big big.

zoegirl: i'm here. spill!

mad maddie: excellent. which do u wanna hear first: maddie and ian get down and dirty OR maddie scores one for the gipper?

zoegirl: ooo, give me the down and dirty.

mad maddie: let me first just say that i would have told u this earlier, like at the crack of dawn when i called our dear friend angela.

zoegirl: the "crack of dawn" being what, around 10:30?

mad maddie: but noooooo, you didn't answer my call, cuz u were off being holy with mr. h.

zoegirl: i'm here now, so tell me!

mad maddie: i dunno. u church types might find what i'm about to say offensive . . .

zoegirl: maddie? i swear i'm going to flush your phone down the toilet if u don't tell me now. i'll reach

	through space, grab your phone, and flush it down.
mad maddie:	hmm. i suppose i'll take pity on u, since i'm older and wiser and know how foolish u youngsters can be.
zoegirl:	TELL ME!
mad maddie:	well there we were, me and ian. we'd gotten off work at around 11, but instead of going anywhere, we decided to hang out in my car— doesn't that have a nice ring? hang out in my car?—and listen to music.
zoegirl:	grooving in the gremlin. nice.
mad maddie:	ian had some watered-down rum and coke left over from a party he'd gone to on friday, and before u get all freaky on me, NO, i didn't have any.
mad maddie:	well, maybe a sip.
zoegirl:	maddie! you JUST got your license, you cannot drink and drive!!!
mad maddie:	a sip, zoe. i barely got my lips wet. ian drank the rest of it, which wasn't that much, but it was enough to, like, loosen him up a little.
zoegirl:	and???
mad maddie:	and it was fun
mad maddie:	it was funny, actually, cuz even with the rum and coke, he was totally shy. he put his arm around me and shifted so that i was leaning against him, my back to his chest, but all he did was kiss the top of my head over and over.
zoegirl:	that's sweet!
mad maddie:	so we didn't really get down and dirty. we got . . . smudged. but it's a start, right?
zoegirl:	absolutely

mad maddie:	and u know what's really awesome? the fact that he goes to a different school.
zoegirl:	huh?
mad maddie:	i know, it's weird. but it's like i can be whoever i wanna be around him, cuz i don't know shit about his school and he doesn't know shit about mine. so none of that garbage gets in the way.
zoegirl:	what garbage? like jana, you mean?
mad maddie:	well, yeah, altho i don't mean just jana. and anywayz, she's not as bad as i thought. but ALL that stuff, all the cliques and hierarchies and in-crowds and out-crowds—i don't have to deal with it when i'm with ian.
zoegirl:	sounds nice
mad maddie:	it is
mad maddie:	and now r u ready for maddie scores one for the gipper?
zoegirl:	who the hell is "the gipper"?
mad maddie:	i have no idea. some football coach? but in this case it's you and angela.
zoegirl:	i'm the gipper? all right. how'd you score one for me?
mad maddie:	u AND angela, i said. yr both the gipper. cuz during brunch yesterday i bit the bullet and talked to my parents about letting us go to cumberland island.
zoegirl:	and . . . ?
mad maddie:	i told them how it's only five hours away, and how we wouldn't do any driving once we got there cuz we'd be camping out on the island, which we'd have to take a ferry to get to.
mad maddie:	i told them about all the research i'd done, which made me sound extremely mature and industrious. i even printed up maps to show

	them. AND i said we might get to see wild horses, which would be, like, an experience of a lifetime.
zoegirl:	wow. are there really wild horses?
mad maddie:	yeah, isn't that cool?
mad maddie:	so anywayz, i told the rents all of this, nodding very calmly and answering their questions, and when we were done talking, they looked at each other and said they'd think about it!!!
zoegirl:	that's awesome!
mad maddie:	now it's up to u and angela. u've got to get going with your parents!
zoegirl:	email me all of that information, the maps and stuff.
mad maddie:	tell them to at least consider it. don't let them give u an answer right away!

Mon, Oct 11, 7:42 PM E.D.T.

SnowAngel:	hey, mads, don't yell at me, ok?
mad maddie:	what r u talking about?
SnowAngel:	i called rob. i just wanted to hear his voice.
mad maddie:	angela!!!
SnowAngel:	but i hung up when he answered. i just didn't know what to say.
SnowAngel:	aren't u gonna respond?
mad maddie:	and say what? u called rob, which was bad. but u hung up before u actually talked to him, which was good, even tho it makes u kinda like a stalker.
SnowAngel:	except then i got worried that he'd see my name on his calls list, so i called right back.
mad maddie:	ANGELA!
SnowAngel:	i was all, "that was so weird! i just called u, but u never answered. is there something wrong with your phone?"
mad maddie:	u asked if there was something wrong with his phone?!!

SnowAngel:	there could have been! phones go screwy all the time.
SnowAngel:	u don't think he thought i was making it up, do u?
mad maddie:	**why no, angela. why on earth would he think that?**
SnowAngel:	anyway, i hoped . . . i dunno. i hoped that when he heard my voice, he'd remember all the fun we'd had and he'd want to get back together.
SnowAngel:	but there was just this really long silence, and then he said, "i'm confused. did u want something?"
SnowAngel:	so don't u have a response?
SnowAngel:	maddie!!!
SnowAngel:	MADDIE, WHERE DID YOU GO?
mad maddie:	**i'm here, sorry. just watching an episode of "family guy"**
SnowAngel:	while i pour out my heart to you???
mad maddie:	**it's called multitasking, and all i can say is, rob's an asshole**
SnowAngel:	i know, but i miss him anyway. it just hurts, maddie. 😟
SnowAngel:	why do these things always happen to ME?
mad maddie:	**that, dearest angela, is a very good question.**

Mon, Oct 11, 7:56 PM E.D.T.

SnowAngel:	i miss rob 😟
zoegirl:	i know. poor angela.
SnowAngel:	do u think i should call him? i called him once already—actually twice—but our convo was kinda weird. maybe i should call him again to straighten things out.
zoegirl:	i don't know, angela. maybe you should wait and talk to him at school.
SnowAngel:	but he never does talk to me! he practically runs down the hall every time he sees me!
zoegirl:	well . . . doesn't that tell u something?

zoegirl:	i don't mean to be harsh
SnowAngel:	fine. screw him. HE'S the one missing out, not me.
zoegirl:	so true. be strong!

Tues, Oct 12, 5:23 PM E.D.T.

SnowAngel:	maddie, u r in big trouble!
SnowAngel:	it was downright chilly walking home from school today—i'm talking serious nipple weather—but i guess u wouldn't know since u were snug and warm IN YOUR CAR. did u sneak off to meet ian? hmm? is that why u forgot to pick me up, cuz u wanted some more of his sweet loving?
mad maddie:	**Angela? This is Madigan's mother. My phone's battery died, and I needed to check if one of my stocks had gone down.**
SnowAngel:	oh, ok. i'm really sorry.
mad maddie:	**Is there something I should know about Madigan and Ian?**
SnowAngel:	no! i was just joking around. i'll get off now, ok?
mad maddie:	**ha ha, gotcha.**
SnowAngel:	shit, maddie! *tries to stop hyperventilating*
mad maddie:	**don't worry, the moms could never use my phone. she doesn't know my password.**
SnowAngel:	U SUCK!!!
mad maddie:	**did u like the correct punctuation, tho? that was a nice touch, i think.**
SnowAngel:	u r a total poopyhead and i hate u.
SnowAngel:	so why DID u forget me?! i waited for 20 minutes and u never showed up!
mad maddie:	**hey, now. i was there at 4 o'clock sharp. U were the one who didn't show.**
SnowAngel:	what? i stopped by the auditorium to find out about drama club sign-up, and then i came right to the parking lot. i was there by 4:05 at the latest.

mad maddie:	well . . . in that case . . . sorry. i'd told jana i'd give her a ride too, and she kinda wanted to get going.
SnowAngel:	EXCUSE me?
mad maddie:	i ran into her after last period. she lives sorta near me, u know.
SnowAngel:	i can't believe u ditched me to give jana whitaker a ride!
mad maddie:	don't have a cow. god.
SnowAngel:	think about it, maddie. first u treat jana like she's the anti-christ, and now all of a sudden—snap!—ur her chauffeur? and not only that, but ur driving HER instead of ME?
mad maddie:	angela, u live five blocks from school. u walk home every day of yr life.
SnowAngel:	that is so not the point and u know it.
mad maddie:	she needed a ride
SnowAngel:	and out of all the ppl in the world, U had to give her one?
mad maddie:	not that many sophomores have cars. i do.
SnowAngel:	omg, ur a car snob! u've had your license for four days and ur already a car snob!
mad maddie:	this is stupid. do u have anything important to say, or did u just wanna rag on me some more?
SnowAngel:	*lifts eyebrows*
mad maddie:	whatevs. i'll give rides to whoever i want, so i wish u wldn't try to guilt-trip me.
SnowAngel:	fine, i won't!

Tues, Oct 12, 5:45 PM E.D.T.

SnowAngel:	i am so pissed at maddie. wanna know why? 😞
SnowAngel:	she gave jana whitaker a ride home instead of me. can u believe that? i was five minutes late to the parking lot, *maybe* ten, and she left without me!
zoegirl:	well, at least u live close to school.

SnowAngel:	but zoe! she left cuz jana told her to, and then she acted like it was no big deal. like it was my problem for getting bent out of shape.
SnowAngel:	jana's buddying up to maddie and making her feel cool, and maddie's totally falling for it. it's sickening. 😠😠😠
zoegirl:	maybe jana had an appointment or something. maybe she had to get home by a certain time.
SnowAngel:	that makes no sense. if jana had anything important to get to, her mom would have picked her up, not maddie.
zoegirl:	i guess. yeah, you're right.
zoegirl:	hey, want to come with me to the junkman's daughter?
SnowAngel:	isn't that a thrift shop? u know i have polyester issues, zoe.
zoegirl:	i just want a good pair of jeans, some really soft, beat-up ones.
SnowAngel:	what for?
zoegirl:	uh . . . to wear? i'm going to a wellspring party this friday. mr. h is going to be there.
SnowAngel:	ohhhhhhh. sure, i'll meet you there.
SnowAngel:	at least i know u'll actually show, unlike SOME ppl i know.

Thu, Oct 14, 10:02 PM E.D.T.

SnowAngel:	oh man. oh man, oh man, oh man.
zoegirl:	hi, angela. "oh man" what?
SnowAngel:	u know how i said i needed a distraction to help me get over rob? well, welcome to recovery, baby, cuz distraction has arrived.
zoegirl:	does this mean—let me just make a wild guess here—that u've found a new crush?
SnowAngel:	it is SUCH a relief to be moving on, i can't even tell u.

zoegirl:	who's the lucky fella?
SnowAngel:	his name's ben. 😍 he's helping out with drama club, and i swear, zo, he is every kinda hot.
zoegirl:	tell me more. 🙂
SnowAngel:	*drools* i think about rob now, and i don't know what i ever saw in him. i mean, sometimes i even wonder if i was just in love with the idea of being in love, u know?
zoegirl:	you don't say
SnowAngel:	but ben. *swoon*
SnowAngel:	he's a drama major at georgia state, and he's getting course credit for being our assistant director. he's got curly brown hair and gorgeous brown eyes.
SnowAngel:	he's got the tiniest bit of a potbelly, but on him it's really cute.
zoegirl:	👍
SnowAngel:	but u wanna know what i really like about him? how intense he is—like he's thinking all these profound thoughts. he's so much more mature than high school guys.
zoegirl:	is he going to work with the drama club for the whole semester?
SnowAngel:	uh huh. he talked to us today about the play we're putting on—which is "The Crucible"—and he said that creating art is the most important thing we can ever do. it was so inspiring.
zoegirl:	are you trying out for a role?
SnowAngel:	hell no, i signed up to do makeup. but that's art too, zoe.
zoegirl:	i know. i think that's great.
SnowAngel:	i'm sooooooo excited. it feels good to have something to be psyched about.
zoegirl:	have u told maddie?
SnowAngel:	no

zoegirl:	why not? ur not still mad at her, r u?
SnowAngel:	u saw her today, laughing at everything jana said. and i HATE that new expression she has. u know the one i'm talking about, right?
zoegirl:	um. no comment.
SnowAngel:	me: "so maddie, what'd ya think of that geometry test?" maddie: "tits, man. i totally aced it."
SnowAngel:	me: "aw, katie's wearing the cutest skirt! i love it!" maddie: "tits. nice skirt, katie!"
SnowAngel:	*rolls eyes and vomits*
zoegirl:	i called her an hour ago to talk about our piano lessons, because mrs. lynch is out of town. i asked if she'd gotten the message, and she was like, "so i don't have to go to my lesson?" and then . . . yeah. she used her new expression. HATE it.
SnowAngel:	have u heard jana call her "the madster" yet?
zoegirl:	oh no!
SnowAngel:	and maddie calls her "the janster." *vomits some more*
zoegirl:	ack
SnowAngel:	at least she hasn't invited jana on our road trip— which actually is kinda amazing.
zoegirl:	oh baloney. jana may be the flavor of the week, but maddie knows who her real friends are.
SnowAngel:	i hope so
SnowAngel:	speaking of the road trip, i broached the topic with my mom, just in a breezy, chatty kinda way, and she said it sounded fun. now i just have to tell her that we seriously wanna go—not hypothetically, but for real.
zoegirl:	that's pretty much where i am too.
zoegirl:	actually, that's not true. i keep MEANING to bring it up, but then i get scared about my mom's reaction and i wimp out.

SnowAngel:	zoe! u HAVE to. thanksgiving break's not that far away!
zoegirl:	i know, i know
SnowAngel:	did u wash your new jeans to get rid of that funky smell?
zoegirl:	i did. they're perfect. i thought about patching the hole in the knee, but i decided not to.
SnowAngel:	sexy miss zoe, stepping out in her sexy new jeans. *prances down the catwalk*
zoegirl:	shut up. i just want to look decent, that's all. not all nerdy like i normally do.
SnowAngel:	u don't look nerdy!
zoegirl:	well, boring then. i definitely look boring.
zoegirl:	hey, want to come home with me tomorrow and do my makeup for the wellspring party?
SnowAngel:	u mean it?! ur finally gonna let me give u a makeover? *jumps up and down and squeals*
zoegirl:	only if you promise not to go crazy.
SnowAngel:	ooo, this is gonna be fabulous. i lurrrrve makeup. 😃
zoegirl:	that's why i finally decided to ask, because you always seem so happy when you're doing your own. i watched you put on your blush last weekend, and you couldn't stop smiling.
SnowAngel:	???
SnowAngel:	wait, i know what ur talking about. that was so i'd apply my blush right, u goof. when u smile, it makes it easier to find the apples of your cheeks.
zoegirl:	oh. i just thought you were really happy.
SnowAngel:	i AM really happy—that i get to do yours. i'll make u a star, baby!

Fri, Oct 15, 4:54 PM E.D.T.

mad maddie: i'm sorry to report that i've discovered a smell worse than period farts.

zoegirl: period farts?

mad maddie: don't play dumb. i'm talking about those wretched farts u get when u have your period, which r totally different from normal farts?

zoegirl: ahem, maddie? i don't like where this is going.

mad maddie: me neither, and i should know cuz i'm the one who—for some INSANE reason—agreed to try mark's disgusting hemp milk with my raisin bran this morning.

zoegirl: HEMP milk? i thought hemp was something you made clothes out of.

mad maddie: apparently u can make big 💩s out of it too. pelt-woman says it's good for your digestive system, and now mark does 2, cuz he has to do everything she does. i wish he would hurry up and move into his own apartment and take his nasty hemp milk with him, cuz DAMN is it gross. u have to shake it before u use it, and sometimes little clots of something gross come floating out.

zoegirl: that is revolting

mad maddie: and now i have the nastiest gas i've ever had in my life. AND i've got a "date" with ian tonight. i'm trying to get it all out now before he picks me up.

zoegirl: a "date," huh? like, a date date?

mad maddie: dinner and a movie, the whole shebang.

zoegirl: maddie, that's so sweet! u've got a real live beau!

mad maddie: until i blow him away with my farts, that is.

mad maddie: hey, if i text angela, is she gonna act all pissy, or has she forgiven me for giving jana a ride home on tuesday?

zoegirl: she's still annoyed, but u should text her anyway. she was just over here, but i bet she's home by now.

mad maddie: why was she over there? were u guys having a secret powwow w/o me?

zoegirl:	relax, she was just teaching me how to do makeup. u would've hated it.
mad maddie:	that's for damn sure
mad maddie:	anyway, the whole jana thing was SO not a big deal. angela made it out like i was picking jana over her, and that totally wasn't the case.
zoegirl:	listen, u don't have to convince me.
mad maddie:	i mean, u and angela r my best friends, that goes without saying. but that doesn't mean i can't be friends with jana 2.
zoegirl:	i'm really ok with this, maddie.
mad maddie:	right. sorry.
mad maddie:	so . . . what r u doing tonight? any big plans now that ur all made up and beautiful?
zoegirl:	tonight? nah. i'll be psyched to hear how your date goes, tho.
mad maddie:	yeah, i'll tell u all about it. guess i better—oops, there goes another one.
zoegirl:	another what?
mad maddie:	another hemp-milk fart. my butt cheeks r still flapping. byeas!

Fri, Oct 15, 5:55 PM E.D.T.

mad maddie:	hola, angela.
mad maddie:	r u still mad at me, or have u realized the error of your ways?
SnowAngel:	???
mad maddie:	never mind. let's talk about something else, like my date with ian. i'm actually kinda nervous. isn't that weird?
SnowAngel:	no. that means u like him!
mad maddie:	i keep wondering if he'll be more aggressive tonight, if he'll go for the gusto and kiss me on the lips and not just the top of my head.

SnowAngel:	do u want him to?
mad maddie:	**i think so, yeah.**
SnowAngel:	first kisses r soooooooo romantic. *sighs*
mad maddie:	**what about u? what r u up to tonight?**
SnowAngel:	NOTHING! *stomps around and kicks things* i feel like such a loser.
mad maddie:	**that sucks**
SnowAngel:	tell me about it. altho it's not SO bad, cuz chrissy and i are going to watch "The Spectacular Now." i luv that movie.
mad maddie:	**tits, man**
SnowAngel:	will u PLEASE stop saying that? that is the dumbest expression i've ever heard. it's like saying, "penis, man," or "testicles. awesome."
mad maddie:	**ooo—aren't we touchy**
mad maddie:	**maybe u shld call zo, see if she wants to come hang with u and chrissy.**
SnowAngel:	well, yeah, i wld, if she didn't have her own hot date. thanks for rubbing it in.
mad maddie:	**zoe has a date?**
SnowAngel:	fine, so it's not technically a "date." it's still more exciting than popcorn and tv.
mad maddie:	**exsqueeze me, but what r u talking about?**
SnowAngel:	that wellspring party zoe's going to. get with the program.
mad maddie:	**zoe's going to a wellspring party? tonight?**
SnowAngel:	r we having a communication problem here? *cups hands around mouth* YES, ZOE'S GOING TO A WELLSPRING PARTY TONIGHT. that's why she got those new jeans she was wearing today, and that's why i went over and dolled her up. she looks totally fab, btw.
mad maddie:	**hold on. i texted zoe like an hour ago, and she said nothing about a wellspring party. i asked**

	her flat-out what she was doing tonight, and she didn't say a word.
SnowAngel:	huh. probably cuz she didn't want u saying, "tits, man."
mad maddie:	**screw u. is mr. h gonna be there?**
SnowAngel:	he's the one who told her about it.
mad maddie:	**what?!!**
mad maddie:	**all right, fine. i can't think about this anymore.**
SnowAngel:	wait a minute—r u upset about this?
mad maddie:	**don't be dumb**
SnowAngel:	cuz u seem upset, and now i'm thinking i shouldn't have said anything.
mad maddie:	**ian's gonna be here soon. i've g2g.**
SnowAngel:	ok, if u say so. have fun!

Fri, Oct 15, 9:09 PM E.D.T.

SnowAngel:	have u drunk the Kool-Aid yet?
zoegirl:	no, and don't be mean. you sound like maddie.
SnowAngel:	well, r u having fun? is the party still going on? it's getting late for the church-going crowd, isn't it?
zoegirl:	hahaha.

Sat, Oct 16, 11:03 AM E.D.T.

zoegirl:	angela! oh, AN-gela!
SnowAngel:	hey!
zoegirl:	just to satisfy your curiosity, yes, the party WAS fun. billy summers brought his guitar, and we did a lot of sing-alongs. maddie would have laughed her head off.
SnowAngel:	what about mr. h? was he there?
zoegirl:	he was
SnowAngel:	and?
zoegirl:	ack. i really should tell u in person. r u still coming over?

SnowAngel:	don't u DARE leave me hanging like that. did something happen with mr. h?!!!
zoegirl:	i don't know. maybe?
SnowAngel:	TELL ME!!!!
zoegirl:	well . . . it was when he gave me a ride home. i was about to call my mom to pick me up, but he said he was ready to go 2.
SnowAngel:	i bet
zoegirl:	so it was just the 2 of us in his car, and at first i felt pretty jumpy. i don't know why, really, except maybe that it was dark out? it made things feel more intimate than the times he took me to church.
SnowAngel:	mmm-hmmm. go on.
zoegirl:	so . . . we talked. and when we got to my house, he cut the engine and we talked a little longer. which shows how innocent it was, cuz my parents were right there, less than 20 feet away.
SnowAngel:	yeah, INSIDE the house
zoegirl:	he said i seem a lot older than 15, and that he's really enjoyed getting to know me. i know it sounds corny, but it was nice.
SnowAngel:	i can c that
zoegirl:	and then . . .
SnowAngel:	what?
zoegirl:	well, he made this comment about my jeans, teasing me about how raggedy they were. and then he reached over and touched the hole, kinda running his finger around the worn part.
SnowAngel:	zoe! OMG!!!
zoegirl:	it was almost like he was doing it as an excuse to touch my leg.
SnowAngel:	well. yeah! cuz he WAS doing it as an excuse to touch your leg!

zoegirl:	but he wasn't being a lech or anything. i don't want u to get the wrong idea.
SnowAngel:	shit. zoe. HE'S YOUR TEACHER!!!
zoegirl:	i know
SnowAngel:	did u like it? ooo—that sounds icky. i mean. was it ok with u that he did that?
zoegirl:	i don't know. i'm not mad or anything, if that's what u mean.
SnowAngel:	*whistles*
zoegirl:	do u think that's awful? do u think it's really gross?
SnowAngel:	r u still gonna go to church with him on sunday?
zoegirl:	uh huh. my mom's baking thumbprint cookies to give him when he picks me up, the kind with jam inside. she, like, adores him.
SnowAngel:	wow
zoegirl:	don't tell anyone any of this, all right? i mean, i know u wouldn't, but i just wanted to make sure.
SnowAngel:	don't worry
SnowAngel:	even if i did, no one would believe me.
zoegirl:	what's that supposed to mean?
SnowAngel:	just that ur so pure and innocent. no one would believe that ur secretly this lady of the night.
zoegirl:	angela!
SnowAngel:	jk
zoegirl:	NOT funny
SnowAngel:	so what time do u want me to come over? i can come right now if u want.
zoegirl:	sure. and hopefully maddie'll drop by after work. ooo, and maybe she can bring some beignets.

Sun, Oct 17, 6:52 PM E.D.T.

| zoegirl: | maddie, where ARE you? i've called half a dozen times, but you never called back. plus you never |

	stopped by last night. what was up with that—were you too busy with ian?
mad maddie:	i'm here, i'm here. chill.
mad maddie:	and ian and i hung out a little, but i was home before 11:00.
zoegirl:	so why didn't you come over?
mad maddie:	i guess i was just worn out. sorry.
zoegirl:	that's okay. but you hung out with ian! yay! did you have fun?
mad maddie:	it was all right
zoegirl:	that's all? just all right?
mad maddie:	yep
zoegirl:	oh. so what are you doing now?
mad maddie:	nothing
zoegirl:	ok-a-a-a-y
zoegirl:	is something wrong, maddie?
mad maddie:	shld there be?
zoegirl:	no, it's just . . .
zoegirl:	we're texting, but we're not *truly* texting, because i'm the only one really saying anything.
mad maddie:	well, sorry to disappoint. guess u'll have to text angela instead.
zoegirl:	huh?
mad maddie:	she's the one you confide in, after all.
zoegirl:	what? maddie, i have no idea what ur talking about.
mad maddie:	right. of course.
mad maddie:	so how was YOUR weekend?
zoegirl:	it was fine. we missed you last night, though.
mad maddie:	i bet. what about friday night? u miss me then?
zoegirl:	maddie, is THAT what this is about?
mad maddie:	me: so what r u up to tonight? u: oh, nothing.
mad maddie:	god, zoe, u lied to my face!
zoegirl:	maddie . . .

mad maddie:	**why did u tell angela and not me?**
zoegirl:	truthfully? because i knew you'd make fun of me, and i'm sick of it.
mad maddie:	**you still should have told me. i HATE it when u and angela have yr stupid little secrets.**
zoegirl:	well, i'm sorry. i didn't mean to hurt your feelings.
mad maddie:	**well, u did**
zoegirl:	i'm sorry. i really am.
zoegirl:	maddie? r u still there?
mad maddie:	**i'm here**
zoegirl:	do u forgive me?
mad maddie:	**no**
mad maddie:	**r u gonna tell me about it, at least?**
zoegirl:	we had pizza and hung out. happy?
mad maddie:	**what about mr. h? angela says that's why u got those new jeans, to get him all hot and bothered.**
zoegirl:	i did not!
mad maddie:	**did he jump your bones?**
zoegirl:	see, maddie? this is the problem. you act offended if i DON'T tell you, but when i DO, all you do is rag on me.
mad maddie:	**i'm not ragging on u. i'm serious. one day he's gonna lure u away and lock u in a sex prison, i'm not kidding.**
zoegirl:	i told you all there is to tell. we sang songs, cherryl ann booth gave a devotional, some of the kids played jeff's dad's pinball machine. the end.
mad maddie:	**sounds dull as nails**
zoegirl:	it was. but hey, you're the one who asked.

Sun, Oct 17, 7:15 PM E.D.T.

mad maddie:	**zoe? u still there?**
zoegirl:	yeah

mad maddie:	i just wanted to say—quickly—that i DID have fun with ian. it was better than all right.
zoegirl:	aw, maddie, that's great.
mad maddie:	i didn't tell u at first cuz u were on my bad list. but then i started thinking, what if somehow ian saw what i said? not that he ever would. but what if he did, and he thought i wasn't into him?
zoegirl:	how would he see?
mad maddie:	he wouldn't. but that's the thing about privacy and phones and the internet, it's just kinda spooky. i mean, everything's out there, u know?
zoegirl:	you're paranoid. the government is not tapping into our texts, and neither is ian.
zoegirl:	but just in case: DON'T WORRY, IAN! MADDIE REALLY DOES LIKE YOU!

Mon, Oct 18, 8:11 PM E.D.T.

SnowAngel:	hey, miss maddie-pie
mad maddie:	hey, angela. how's tricks?
SnowAngel:	just another day in sophomore paradise. *hums and floats about room*
mad maddie:	wld this have to do with drama club, per chance? old what's-his-name the college guy has made quite an impression, i see.
SnowAngel:	his name's ben. *sighs* ben schlanker.
mad maddie:	ben schlanker? as in schlong + wanker?
SnowAngel:	oh god, maddie. plz.
mad maddie:	schlanker. that's hysterical. if u get married, u'll be angela schlanker.
SnowAngel:	damn u. WHY do u plant these things in my head?!!
mad maddie:	or i suppose u could hyphenate. then u'd be angela silver-schlanker.
SnowAngel:	enough about the name. *glares*
SnowAngel:	do u wanna hear how wonderful he is or not?

mad maddie:	i'd rather make fun of his name some more.
SnowAngel:	he's Jewish, maddie. "schlanker" is a nice, normal Jewish name, and ur being racist.
mad maddie:	sccchhlllanker. hahahahahahahahahahaha.
SnowAngel:	ANYWAY, today ben told us that u have to claw to live, that suffering is what life is all about. isn't that cool?
mad maddie:	u have to *claw* to live?
SnowAngel:	he said suffering brings things into focus. most ppl go la-la-la-ing along for all of their lives, he said, but artists have to stay sharp. we can't be afraid to embrace pain.
mad maddie:	so i suppose u'll be plucking eyebrows, then? applying lots of hot-wax facials?
SnowAngel:	huh?
mad maddie:	ur the makeup girl. ur in a prime position to help the actors embrace as much pain as possible.
SnowAngel:	u just don't get it, do u? oh well. yr loss.
mad maddie:	does this ben guy even know your name?
SnowAngel:	YES he knows my name. today he said something about adam lancaster needing a scar, and he glanced at me and said, "which angela'll take care of, right, angela?"
mad maddie:	does he have a girlfriend?
SnowAngel:	*growls*
mad maddie:	does that mean yes?
SnowAngel:	he talks about some leslie chick a lot. apparently she goes to GA State with him. but maybe she's just a friend.
mad maddie:	uh huh. good luck with that!

Tues, Oct 19, 10:23 PM E.D.T.

mad maddie:	i gave jana a ride home again today—don't tell angela.

zoegirl: lovely

zoegirl: how is ol' jana?

mad maddie: she's good. she cracks me up, all the crazy things she's done. she's actually been cow-tipping, can u believe that? 🐮

zoegirl: no. where'd she find a cow in atlanta? and even if she did, that's mean.

mad maddie: it's not mean. it's funny. but anywayz, she has this awesome idea for how to make a statement about how dumb the speed limit is. wanna hear it?

zoegirl: i suppose

mad maddie: well, u know how EVERYONE drives over 65, right? which makes it totally pointless to even have a speed limit. i mean, seriously. we shld be like germany where everyone just drives at their own speed.

zoegirl: that's jana's statement? be like germany?

mad maddie: hold yer horses. here's her idea: we're gonna get a bunch of ppl to drive out to I-285. we'll have at least 4 cars, 1 for each lane, and we'll work it so that we're all right next to each other.

mad maddie: then we'll set our speed at EXACTLY 65 mph, all at the same time. we'll TOTALLY block traffic. won't that be awesome?!!

zoegirl: i don't get it. how will you block traffic by going 65 mph?

mad maddie: cuz no one goes 65 mph! but this time they'll have to cuz no one will be able to pass us!

zoegirl: you've got to be kidding

zoegirl: you're not actually gonna do this, r u?

mad maddie: hell, yeah. it's brilliant. 💡

zoegirl: haven't you heard of road rage? you're gonna get shot!

mad maddie: that's ridiculous

mad maddie:	i thought you would get it, since you care about issues and stuff.
zoegirl:	important issues, not rebelling against the speed limit.
mad maddie:	whatevs. we're doing it this friday during rush hour if u wanna come.
zoegirl:	have you heard anything i've just said? NO, i don't want to come. it makes me nervous just thinking about it.
mad maddie:	yeah, isn't it great? that's what i love about jana. when i'm with her, i get this excitement inside of me and an "i'm ready to do anything" attitude. it scares the shit out of me.
zoegirl:	and you like that?
mad maddie:	i love it
mad maddie:	speaking of excitement—have u asked your parents about cumberland island yet? u keep saying ur gonna, and then u never do!
zoegirl:	oh! i DID ask them, and they pretty much said no freakin way. mom's exact words were "three 15-year-olds alone on the highway? are you out of your mind?"
mad maddie:	hey! i'm 16!!!
zoegirl:	i told her that. it didn't make any difference.
mad maddie:	did u beg and plead and throw a fit?
zoegirl:	they're not going to go for it, mads. it sucks, but they're just not.
mad maddie:	well, i'm gonna figure something out. i'm not giving up yet!

Wed, Oct 20, 7:14 PM E.D.T.

mad maddie:	i am on a hot streak, ladies. a hot streak, i'm telling u! 🔥 🔥 🔥
SnowAngel:	you are?

zoegirl:	tell us what's going on!
mad maddie:	yay! ur both here. good girls for being textable *pats friends on heads*
mad maddie:	SO. i talked to the moms again about our cumberland island trip, and guess what she said?!!!
SnowAngel:	what?
mad maddie:	well . . . she and the pops agree with zoe's mom that it's not a good idea for us to go by ourselves, cuz she's worried we'd get a flat or pick up a hitchhiker or something. whatevs.
mad maddie:	so i said "what if mark and erin came 2?" and she talked it over with pops, and they said YES!
zoegirl:	erin? who's erin?
mad maddie:	mark's girlfriend. pelt-woman. i made mark call her right then, and she's all for it. wild horses, camping, remote little island—it's totally up her alley.
SnowAngel:	maddie, that's AWESOME! 😃
zoegirl:	it is. it totally is. but wouldn't it be weird, the three of us plus mark and erin?
mad maddie:	no, and here's why. we'll tail each other down there, but mark and erin'll have their own car and we'll have ours.
mad maddie:	once we get to the island, we won't even have to see them. we can camp wherever we want, and so can they.
SnowAngel:	maddie, ur brilliant. now we just have to convince my parents and zoe's parents.
zoegirl:	oh no. i'm going to be the one person who doesn't get to go. i just know it.
mad maddie:	remind them that mark and erin r both 21, and we'll be with them the whole time. (we really won't, but they don't have to know that. shhhh . . .)

mad maddie:	also tell them they can call u whenever they want.
mad maddie:	we HAVE to make it happen, you guys. it's important. cuz sometimes i feel like we're drifting away from each other, and we can't let that happen.
SnowAngel:	we r not drifting away from each other. what r u talking about?
SnowAngel:	if anyone's drifting away, it's U
mad maddie:	wtf?
zoegirl:	you're not drifting away, don't worry. NO ONE is drifting away.
mad maddie:	cuz for the record, i am the one person who has stayed exactly the same. u two r the ones changing, not me.
SnowAngel:	change of subject: who wants to go bowling with me on friday? 🎳
SnowAngel:	doug schmidt asked me to go, and i couldn't bear to turn him down. but i don't want it to be a date-type thing, so i told him i'd see if anyone else wanted to come along.
zoegirl:	he wants to go BOWLING? that's so cute!
mad maddie:	hold on. doug schmidt asked u out—for the forty millionth time—and u said, "sure, and hey, here's a thought: why don't i bring my friends along?"
SnowAngel:	it's better than saying no, isn't it?
mad maddie:	not much
SnowAngel:	so will you come? please, please, please?
mad maddie:	can't, sorry
SnowAngel:	why not?
mad maddie:	i've got plans
SnowAngel:	with ian?
mad maddie:	with some ppl from school
zoegirl:	some people from school? could you be more vague?

SnowAngel:	omg. do u have plans with JANA?
zoegirl:	she does. dangerous stupid plans that could get her killed or arrested or flattened on the highway.
mad maddie:	**thanks, zo**
zoegirl:	it's true!
SnowAngel:	*stomps foot* somebody better tell me RIGHT NOW what ur doing with jana!
mad maddie:	**we're doing a social psychology experiment. it's no big deal.**
SnowAngel:	what kind of "social psychology experiment"? what IS a social psychology experiment?
zoegirl:	yes, maddie. please educate us.
mad maddie:	**screw you both. i say that in the nicest possible way, but really.**
mad maddie:	**screw you.**
SnowAngel:	maddie, why r u so mad?
SnowAngel:	maddie!
SnowAngel:	where'd she go? I AM SO CONFUSED.
SnowAngel:	zoe, wld u plz tell me what just happened?
zoegirl:	i'm going to let her tell you. I don't mean to add to the drama. it's just, i want HER to see YOUR reaction when you first hear, not after you've already had it explained to you.
SnowAngel:	zoe?
zoegirl:	yes?
SnowAngel:	um, that totally adds to the drama.
zoegirl:	tell you what. if i go bowling with you and doug, will that make it up to u?
SnowAngel:	no. yes. i don't know.
SnowAngel:	but thx at least for that.

Thu, Oct 21, 5:51 PM E.D.T.

SnowAngel:	zo! i told doug ur coming with us on friday and he's psyched. 👍

zoegirl:	er . . . actually . . .
SnowAngel:	doug's gonna ask steve brinks to come too. it can be like a double date!
zoegirl:	aaiee. i can't go after all, angela. don't hate me! *cringes in corner*
SnowAngel:	WHAT?
SnowAngel:	is it cuz of the double-date thing? doug really is gonna invite steve, but it doesn't have to be a double date. it can just be a group of friends.
zoegirl:	it's not that. it's just that i stayed for mr. h's backwork today, and he kind of asked if i wanted to play bingo with him on friday night.
SnowAngel:	WHAT?!!!
zoegirl:	not just the two of us—his mother'll be there too. she lives in a nursing home, and once a month they have bingo night.
zoegirl:	he asked if i wanted to go.
SnowAngel:	let me get this straight: ur ditching me to play bingo with mr. h and his mother?
zoegirl:	please don't hate me. it's just that i kind of forgot about our bowling plans till it was too late. and . . . i don't want to tell mr. h no.
SnowAngel:	i don't get it. how can mr. h ask u to go play bingo with him as if it's a totally normal thing? doesn't he know ur his student?
zoegirl:	we'll be with a bunch of old people, angela. i think it's really sweet.
SnowAngel:	*shakes head* unbelievable
zoegirl:	but, on the other hand, he wants me to meet his mother. that's kind of a big deal . . . isn't it?
SnowAngel:	it's kind of INSANE
SnowAngel:	have u told maddie?
zoegirl:	just you
SnowAngel:	good, cuz maddie would have a heyday.

zoegirl:	r u mad?
SnowAngel:	yes *sticks out tongue*
SnowAngel:	but i suppose i'll forgive u eventually.
zoegirl:	thank you, thank you, thank you
SnowAngel:	EVENTUALLY, i said. right now i'm gonna call megan and kristin and c if either of them can go. or i'll tell maddie that she has to forget that idiotic driving thing and be my escort since u turned traitor.
zoegirl:	so she told you?
zoegirl:	i thought it was weird how at first she didn't want you to know.
SnowAngel:	did she actually say "please don't tell angela"?
zoegirl:	pretty much
SnowAngel:	how annoying
zoegirl:	she gets hurt if i tell u something and not her— like about that wellspring party—but she thinks it's fine to tell me stuff and not u.
SnowAngel:	so what was the deal, did she think i'd disapprove cuz it involved jana?
zoegirl:	something like that
SnowAngel:	well, i *do* disapprove, and that's even more reason she should ditch jana and come with me. anyway, i need her more than jana does.
SnowAngel:	i'm gonna text her and tell her that now. i hope she listens.

Thu, Oct 21, 6:13 PM E.D.T.

SnowAngel:	maddie! oh, maaaaddie!
mad maddie:	**yes?**
SnowAngel:	u have to listen to what i'm about to say. now i know ur all excited about your ridiculous speed limit thingie, but u HAVE to change your plans. ok? ok. great!
mad maddie:	**huh? what?**

SnowAngel:	stupid zoe backed out on me. U CAN'T LEAVE ME ALONE WITH DOUG!!!
mad maddie:	sorry, doll. if i don't go with jana, they won't have enough drivers.
SnowAngel:	but this is important!
mad maddie:	so is this. jana's counting on me. she's gonna ride in my car and everything. hey, i know—forget doug and come with us!
SnowAngel:	i can't, that would be cruel. plus, he already invited steve brinks to come too.
mad maddie:	u, doug, and steve, hmmm? ooh-la-la.
SnowAngel:	*stomps foot* this is serious!
mad maddie:	oh, it is not. invite some other girl to come.
SnowAngel:	i already tried megan AND kristin AND mary kate, and they're all busy. uʀ my only hope, obi-one kenobi!!!
mad maddie:	i'm pretty sure that's not how u spell it, but points for making a star wars reference at all.
mad maddie:	i'm not gonna break my word to jana. sorry. but luckily, i have just the thing to cheer u up.
SnowAngel:	what?
mad maddie:	it's the "my little pony" quiz! after 15 long years u can finally find out which little pony u r! 🐎
SnowAngel:	i'm having a crisis, and u want me to take one of your stupid quizzes?!! no thx.
mad maddie:	why, r u scared?
SnowAngel:	scared of what?
mad maddie:	scared that my inner dragon might eat your little pony?
SnowAngel:	omg. u've been waiting to say that, haven't u? u've been, like, really excited to use that line.
mad maddie:	cuz it's funny. admit it.
SnowAngel:	u r no help at all.
mad maddie:	but i'm amusing, which is even better!

zoegirl:	mr. h is gonna be here any minute . . . but i just wanted to give u moral support before your date.
SnowAngel:	it's not a date!!!
zoegirl:	right, right. sorry.
SnowAngel:	change your mind and come with me. plz????
zoegirl:	i can't. i already told u!
SnowAngel:	*pouts*
SnowAngel:	do i have time to tell u what i'm wearing, at least?
zoegirl:	go for it
SnowAngel:	attire: baggy overalls with long-sleeved white t-shirt underneath (NOT tight), fugly "sensible" shoes my mom made me buy when we went hiking last summer, hair in ponytail.
zoegirl:	baggy overalls and a ponytail. are you trying to send a message here, by any chance?
SnowAngel:	i am being polite to doug. i see no reason to get him all worked up for nothing.
zoegirl:	how considerate.
zoegirl:	well, seriously, have fun.

Sat, Oct 23, 1:52 PM E.D.T.

mad maddie:	**woo-eee! i'm at starbucks and i'm on my fifth breve bomb cuz i was already so wired i figged i might as well add to the adrenaline.**
SnowAngel:	yr fifth . . . ?
SnowAngel:	what's a breve bomb?
mad maddie:	**not important. ready to hear about my fabulous I-285 adventure?**
SnowAngel:	no, cuz i wanna tell u something first. MY PARENTS SAID YES ABOUT CUMBERLAND ISLAND!!!
mad maddie:	**no way!**
SnowAngel:	way! as long as mark and erin will be there to "chaperone" us, they said i could go. *punches the

air in wild excitement* i can't believe they actually said yes!

mad maddie: angela, that is awesome. we r gonna have so much fun!

SnowAngel: i know!!!

SnowAngel: what about zoe's parents—any word?

mad maddie: her mom's gonna call my mom. that's a step, anywayz.

SnowAngel: i agree

mad maddie: and now, onto my account of our exciting and dramatic speed limit rebellion.

SnowAngel: rebellion? i thought u guys were gonna stick to the speed limit exactly. i thought that was the whole point.

mad maddie: the point was to rebel AGAINST the speed limit by showing how dumb it is—which we totally did. oh man, angela, it was wild.

SnowAngel: fine, tell me.

mad maddie: we spread out across I-285 like we planned, each of us in our own lane. then todd spencer gave the thumbs-up, which was the signal for everyone to set their speed to 65 mph. so we did. man, u shoulda seen the look on the face of the guy behind us as he realized he wasn't just behind one slow car, he was behind a whole row of slow cars.

SnowAngel: was he pissed?

mad maddie: more like confused . . . for a few moments. and then it was really funny, cuz slowly the stretch of highway in front of us emptied out, since the drivers ahead of us were driving faster than 65, and then EVERYONE ELSE was stuck behind us. 🚗 🚗 🚗 🚗

SnowAngel: wow

mad maddie: a couple of ppl honked their horns, and then a couple more, and then *everyone* was honking and it was the loudest noise i've ever heard. it was cool, but i actually started getting a little freaked out.

SnowAngel: i TOLD u it was dangerous!

mad maddie: i mean, i could FEEL the fury directed at us. it was like a mob was forming or something.

SnowAngel: *shivers*

mad maddie: then cars started passing us in the emergency lane. kaitlin jones was the driver in the far right lane—the one next to the emergency lane—and i was SO glad it wasn't me. this one car whizzed past her, blaring its horn, and then pulled into her lane so closely that he almost cropped her bumper.

SnowAngel: shit, maddie

mad maddie: then someone threw a beer bottle at joe weiss's car. it made a loud crack, like a gun, and i about crapped my pants.

SnowAngel: did it actually HIT joe's car?

mad maddie: no, thank god

mad maddie: by this time cars were passing in the left-hand emergency lane too. this one guy in a volvo pulled right in front of rex and terri and jana and then intentionally slammed on his brakes. can u believe that?

SnowAngel: omg, maddie. u guys r sooooooo lucky no one got hurt.

mad maddie: then kaitlin broke out of formation, cuz i guess she lost her nerve, which meant more cars could get through.

mad maddie: after that, the rest of us fell out of line too. at first ppl glared and shouted stuff out their windows

	as they passed, but soon they must not have recognized us, cuz no one did anything *truly* terrible.
SnowAngel:	u could have been killed, maddie.
mad maddie:	**but i wasn't.**
SnowAngel:	but u COULD have been.
mad maddie:	**the only thing i'm bummed about is that we didn't make it onto the news. think how great it wld have been when they announced it: "cars going the speed limit cause traffic jam"!**
SnowAngel:	hey, wait a sec. that car that slammed on his brakes . . .
SnowAngel:	i just scrolled back to read that text. did u say he pulled out in front of rex, terri, and jana?
mad maddie:	**yeah, what an asshole. it was really scary.**
SnowAngel:	i thought jana was gonna ride with u.
mad maddie:	**well, she ended up riding with rex and terri instead.**
SnowAngel:	so who rode with u?
mad maddie:	**no one**
SnowAngel:	u were out there with a bunch of maniacs behind u BY YOURSELF?
mad maddie:	**it was no big deal, angela.**
SnowAngel:	was anyone else alone, like kaitlin or joe?
mad maddie:	**what's yr point?**
SnowAngel:	they weren't, were they? u were the only one without a passenger.
mad maddie:	**i SAID it was no big deal. ur making it out like . . . i dunno, like jana did some horrible thing by riding with rex instead of me. but i was the one who was there, so i get to choose if it was a problem or not. AND IT WASN'T.**
SnowAngel:	it just doesn't seem very nice, that's all.
mad maddie:	**ur totally reading into it.**

mad maddie:	anywayz, unlike some ppl, i'm fine being by myself. i don't need reassurance 24-7.
SnowAngel:	what is that supposed to mean?
mad maddie:	u figure it out.
SnowAngel:	u know what, maddie?
SnowAngel:	nvm
mad maddie:	what? go ahead and say it.
SnowAngel:	it's just that all our convos seem to end this way these days, and it's getting really annoying. ur always getting huffy over nothing.
mad maddie:	I'M the one getting huffy?
SnowAngel:	well, i'm glad u had fun with your new friends, even tho none of them actually wanted to be in the same car with u.
mad maddie:	what a lovely thing to say. and i'm glad that you're not AT ALL threatened by the fact that i'm hanging out with jana just cuz jana's in a different social league than u.
mad maddie:	i'm sorry if ur jealous, angela, but don't take it out on me.
SnowAngel:	what?!! u r insane if u think i'm jealous of jana whitaker.
mad maddie:	am i?

Sat, Oct 23, 2:19 PM E.D.T.

SnowAngel:	zoe! aaargh!!!!!!!!
SnowAngel:	i just had the most infuriating convo with maddie!
zoegirl:	what happened?
SnowAngel:	she was bragging about her 285 adventure—that's what started it. i happened to mention that i didn't think it was very nice that no one rode with her, not even her precious jana, and she totally flipped out and got nasty.
SnowAngel:	god, zoe, it is so weird with her these days! one

	minute things r fine and dandy, and then the next minute we're at each other's throats!
zoegirl:	maybe it's weird just because she knows you don't like jana.
SnowAngel:	well, she shouldn't either. jana sucks. she's just using maddie for her car—it's so obvious.
zoegirl:	is it?
SnowAngel:	YES
zoegirl:	i don't know. the whole scene sounded sketchy to me, like a bunch of obnoxious high school kids on a power trip. i'm glad i wasn't there.
SnowAngel:	me too
zoegirl:	how about your night? how'd bowling go?
SnowAngel:	and that's another thing! maddie didn't even bother to ask about that, thank u very much. it's like she thinks my life is too boring to talk about.
zoegirl:	well, I'M asking: how was it hanging out with doug and steve? was it fun, or was it miserable?
SnowAngel:	*does wishy-washy thing with hand*
zoegirl:	explain
SnowAngel:	it wasn't soooooo bad. i got chrissy to come with me at the very last minute, and it was surprisingly fun having her along.
SnowAngel:	she kept getting gutter balls, and one time the ball flew off her hand when she was swinging it backward. it bounced across the floor making these big whomping sounds, and we all cracked up.
zoegirl:	chrissy's great. if i had a sister, i'd want one like chrissy.
SnowAngel:	yeah. she looked really good too. she wore a pair of jeans with embroidery at the bottom, along with a pink t-shirt that said "princess" on it. which sounds dreadful, but on her it looked cute.
zoegirl:	did doug and steve hit on her? jk

SnowAngel:	*arches one eyebrow* actually . . .
zoegirl:	**angela! she's 12!!!**
SnowAngel:	they didn't hit on her, exactly.
zoegirl:	**then what?**
SnowAngel:	well, like i said, chrissy kept throwing gutter balls, and each time she would laugh and get embarrassed and say she was never gonna go bowling again.
SnowAngel:	then one time she went up for her turn, and when she put her fingers in the ball, she stopped and looked confused.
zoegirl:	**why?**
SnowAngel:	there was a note rolled up in one of the holes! she pulled it out, and it said, "ur doing terrific. don't give up. p.s. i think ur pretty."
zoegirl:	**awww!**
zoegirl:	**i take it doug or steve slipped it in there?**
SnowAngel:	yes, but for the longest time they didn't admit it. they said it must be from someone at the bowling alley, one of the guys who worked behind the lanes.
SnowAngel:	chrissy's eyes got big, and she blushed like crazy. then she got even more embarrassed when she rolled a gutter ball again, cuz she was worried that the guy—whoever he was—was watching.
zoegirl:	**that totally makes me like doug and steve. what a sweet thing to do.**
SnowAngel:	yeah, they kept teasing her about it, saying she had a secret admirer and stuff like that.
SnowAngel:	only . . .
zoegirl:	**what?**
SnowAngel:	this is really, really, really humiliating, but i kind of got the teeniest bit jealous. *hides head in shame* this was before i knew doug and steve had planted the note. i kept thinking, "why's that bowling guy flirting with chrissy and not me?"

zoegirl:	silly angela
SnowAngel:	i know. the thought even crossed my mind that the note had been meant for me, and that chrissy had gotten it by accident. how lame, to be jealous of my 12-year-old sister.
zoegirl:	but you were happy for her too, so that's okay. and doug and steve probably wanted to slip notes in your bowling ball, but they knew they couldn't, because that would be, like, too real.
SnowAngel:	*big mushy hug* thanks, zo. u always make me feel better.
SnowAngel:	and last but not least: how was your bingo date with mr. h?
zoegirl:	my wild night at the nursing home? just kidding. 😊
zoegirl:	it was nice. really nice. i helped all these old ppl with their cards, and it made me feel floaty inside.
SnowAngel:	floaty?
zoegirl:	you know, like when you see a sunset, or when you're outside looking at the stars. that huge, happy feeling like you're connected to all the good things in the world.
SnowAngel:	wow. that's awesome.
zoegirl:	it made me want to do more stuff like that, stuff that doesn't involve school and grades and all that pressure. they have a volunteer program, and i'm thinking about signing up.
SnowAngel:	what about mr. h—did anything happen with him?
zoegirl:	well . . . you have to promise not to tell anyone, okay? not even maddie. (and unlike maddie, i honestly mean it.)
SnowAngel:	i promise, i promise! did he kiss you?!! 😲
zoegirl:	no, no, no, nothing like that. but—and i'm probably wrong, and i know i'll sound super

arrogant for even saying this—but i'm starting to think that maybe there could be something between us, something more than the fact that he's my teacher.

SnowAngel: what do u mean?

zoegirl: i think maybe he . . . you know. likes me.

SnowAngel: well, duh, zoe. u don't see mr. miklos schmoozing me for bingo dates, now do u? *shudders* ew, what a horrible image.

zoegirl: you don't think i'm being ridiculous? you think there's, like, a chance?

SnowAngel: do u WANT there to be a chance?

zoegirl: i don't know.

zoegirl: maybe?

zoegirl: oh, wow, i'm turning bright red just saying it out loud—and i'm NOT even saying it out loud. thank goodness we're not talking in person. i'd probably faint.

SnowAngel: whoa. this is so . . . lifetime-channel-ish.

zoegirl: gee, thanks

SnowAngel: no, it's just that u expect things like this to happen in movies, not in real life. only it IS happening in real life.

zoegirl: kind of scary, huh?

SnowAngel: i guess i thought it was just a game, something we talked about just for fun. but ur seriously falling for him, aren't u?

zoegirl: i don't know. i think about him a lot. more than a lot. and last night, when he dropped me off . . .

SnowAngel: yes?

zoegirl: we were sitting in his car, talking, and he reached over and brushed my hair off my face. i know that sounds like nothing, but the way he did it made it seem like more.

SnowAngel:	like how?
zoegirl:	just really gentle, like it meant something to be touching me.
SnowAngel:	wow
zoegirl:	then he pulled back his hand and said, "you're in 10th grade, zoe." and i said, "i know." then he said, "you're 15," and i said, "i know."
SnowAngel:	oh man. he was totally, like, admitting he was into u.
zoegirl:	then he pushed back my hair again, tucking it behind my ear, and . . .
zoegirl:	it's the way he looked at me, like he was saying two different things at the same time.
zoegirl:	it sounds really stupid, doesn't it?
SnowAngel:	it doesn't sound stupid, zo. it sounds . . . big.
zoegirl:	yeah. that's kind of how it feels too.
SnowAngel:	i guess i'm excited for u, since u like him back and everything. but r u sure this is ok? i mean, he's a TEACHER.
zoegirl:	i know. and probably nothing more will happen, not till i graduate. and that won't be for another two years.
SnowAngel:	true. and i've gotta say—thank god for that!

Mon, Oct 25, 7:17 PM E.D.T.

zoegirl:	i saw you drive by my house this afternoon. why didn't you stop?
mad maddie:	i couldn't, cuz i was already running late. i honked, tho.
zoegirl:	yeah, i heard. what were you late for?
mad maddie:	doc appointment. annual physical.
zoegirl:	and?
mad maddie:	no shots, baby!
zoegirl:	wh-hoo!
mad maddie:	at the end, the doctor got all serious and asked

me a bunch of questions. doc: "r u sexually active?" me: "sadly, no." doc: "do u ever drink?" me: "ummm . . ." doc: "have u ever thought of killing yourself?" me: "maybe. doesn't everyone?"

zoegirl: good one

mad maddie: doc: "yes, well, have u ever made a plan?" me: "no, unless continuing to sit through geometry counts as a plan." doc: "excuse me?" me: "meet mr. miklos and u'll understand. u'll die of boredom."

zoegirl: you did not say that.

mad maddie: maybe i did, maybe i didn't. i am a woman of mystery.

zoegirl: speaking of mystery, you have to tell me about you and ian! you started to tell me in homeroom, and then ms. andrist got all busy with announcements.

mad maddie: our saturday night snuggle-fest, u mean?

zoegirl: has he kissed u yet—a real kiss?

mad maddie: he STILL hasn't! he's, like, the snuggle king, which is nice, but i'm ready for more. i keep telling myself that i should make the move myself, but i keep chickening out.

zoegirl: he's probably nervous too

mad maddie: i guess. on saturday, we ended the night with a hug.

zoegirl: awww!

mad maddie: awww, yourself. i'm a growing girl. i have needs, dammit!

zoegirl: he'll get there, just give him time.

mad maddie: or i cld put on crotchless panties and do a lap dance for him.

zoegirl: um. no.

mad maddie: i know that makes me sound like a skank—and i really don't mean it like that. and i'm not pulling an angela, either, like "ooo, he's THE ONE." it's just that ian's awesome, and i want things to get deeper, u know? and if things got more physical, maybe that would happen.

zoegirl: i know what you mean

mad maddie: you do?

zoegirl: i'm not a saint, maddie

mad maddie: well . . . it's different, tho.

zoegirl: how?

mad maddie: cuz with mr. h, u know it'll never go further than a crush, which is totally not the same thing.

zoegirl: maybe it is

mad maddie: and maybe it isn't.

mad maddie: but the moms *definitely* has meatloaf on the table, and it's calling my name!

Tues, Oct 26, 7:30 PM E.D.T.

mad maddie: hey, angela. r u home yet?

SnowAngel: still at drama club. and why do you say "yet"?

mad maddie: cuz it seems like u've been at drama club for an awfully long time.

mad maddie: how's the schlanker?

SnowAngel: BEN is superb, thanks for asking. he told me a funny story about something that happened at starbucks. wanna hear?

mad maddie: the schlank-master goes to starbucks? i'd figure him for aurora or churchill grounds, one of those coffee joints where he could snap his fingers and wear a black beret.

SnowAngel: *narrows eyes* do not make fun of the schlank-master—i mean BEN!!! do u wanna hear the story or not?

mad maddie: by all means

SnowAngel: he was sitting in starbucks reading the newspaper when this frat boy came up and asked if he could look at the sports section. ben handed it to him and said, "sure, i don't read that section anyway." then the frat boy snorted and said, "yeah, i kinda figured."

mad maddie: **asshole**

SnowAngel: so ben stood up, took the paper out of the guy's hands, and said, "yr reading privileges have been revoked. sorry!"

mad maddie: **ha! that's awesome**

SnowAngel: i know. he is my hero.

mad maddie: **tits, man**

SnowAngel: please

SnowAngel: hey, do u know what i just realized on the way home from school? HALLOWEEN IS LESS THAN A WEEK AWAY! what r we gonna do this year? r we gonna go trick-or-treating?

mad maddie: **hell, yeah. free candy!**

SnowAngel: u don't think we're too old?

mad maddie: **let's try this again: FREE CANDY!!!**

SnowAngel: well, what should we go as?

mad maddie: **let me think about it. do u care if i invite ian?**

SnowAngel: sure, if u think he'd wanna come. he has to come up with his own costume, tho. he can't glom onto us.

mad maddie: **i'll swing the idea by him and see what he says.**
🎃

Tues, Oct 26, 7:46 PM E.D.T.

SnowAngel: yay! i just had a convo with maddie and it was NORMAL!!!

zoegirl: wh-hoo!

SnowAngel: i know. i've been like trying really hard to be cool around her, but at school it's impossible cuz she's always tagging after jana. *barf* but our text just now was totally fine. i'm so glad! 😀

zoegirl: that's awesome.

SnowAngel: yup, and that's all i've got. bye!

Wed, Oct 27, 5:33 PM E.D.T.

zoegirl: guess what?!! MOM AND DAD SAID I CAN GO TO CUMBERLAND ISLAND!!!

mad maddie: r u yanking my chain?

zoegirl: no, they really did! i almost had them sign a piece of paper swearing they wouldn't change their minds, but i thought that might be pushing it.

mad maddie: zoe!!! 😀

mad maddie: how did this happen?!!

zoegirl: remember how i told u my mom thought i needed to spend winter break doing something productive?

mad maddie: your mom is such a type A

zoegirl: yeah, cuz she has to be. that's how she gets everything done.

zoegirl: anyway, i thought about it all day, how i could make our trip "productive," and when i got home from school i called a park ranger.

zoegirl: first i talked to him, and then i gave the phone to mom, and he must have been ultra-convincing, because now mom's all fired up about my going on an "environmentalist" adventure. she thinks i'll be able to use it in my college essays.

mad maddie: do they know i'm bringing my mini-tv?

zoegirl: i left that part out, as well as the part about the collapsible chaise lounges. the point is I CAN GO!!!

mad maddie: wh-hoo! cumberland island, here we come!

zoegirl: and in only four weeks!

mad maddie:	which means we have to kick into maximum planning mode, like what kinda food to bring and stuff like that. and we'll have to get our camping gear ready. u DO have a sleeping bag, right?
zoegirl:	i do
mad maddie:	a real one, not one with the little mermaid on it?
zoegirl:	a real one, don't worry.
mad maddie:	good, cuz angela's already borrowing my pops'.
zoegirl:	ha
mad maddie:	hey—i found a great website for u. it's called <u>jesus.com</u>.
zoegirl:	maddie . . .
mad maddie:	i'm not kidding. i feel bad that i've teased u so much, so i've started doing my own religious exploration.
zoegirl:	uh huh, right
mad maddie:	i'm serious. swear to god. just check it out and u'll see!

	Wed, Oct 27, 5:51 PM E.D.T.
zoegirl:	o-k-a-a-a-ay. nice, mads. real nice.
mad maddie:	hi, zoe! *waves*
zoegirl:	*Young women interested in bathing with Jesus can now have their dream come true?!!*
mad maddie:	hee, hee
zoegirl:	*Shower can be exchanged for bubble bath upon request?!!!*
mad maddie:	i'd go for the bubble bath. definitely more romantic.
zoegirl:	you sent me to a porn site!!! WHY did i believe for a second that you were serious?
mad maddie:	i have no idea
mad maddie:	but it's not a porn site. it's a dating service. don't tell me u'd turn down a date with jesus.

zoegirl:	that guy is not jesus! that guy is a psycho!!!
mad maddie:	**so u didn't take the compatibility quiz?**
zoegirl:	omigosh, did YOU?
mad maddie:	**u bet your bootie. it said, You scored in the lowest tenth percentile. You probably don't know what kind of woman Jesus is looking for.**
zoegirl:	well, *that's* true.
mad maddie:	**i took it for u too, since i knew u wouldn't have the balls. or the ovaries. whatevs.**
mad maddie:	**wanna hear your results?**
zoegirl:	no!
mad maddie:	**right on! here goes: You scored above average. Hopefully you don't live too far away. When you contact Jesus, please mention that you are quiz taker #1026747910-29730.**
zoegirl:	oh. my. god.
mad maddie:	**that's the spirit!**
zoegirl:	i don't believe you, maddie.
mad maddie:	**did u see the part about how he gets to take a picture of u in the bubble bath and post it on his website? IF u go out with him, that is.**
zoegirl:	crap
zoegirl:	he's gonna track us both down and murder us.
mad maddie:	**or at least wash our feet. i sent jana a text about the site, and she thought it was hilarious.**
zoegirl:	wait a minute—u and jana have started texting?
mad maddie:	**u say it like i've started using heroin.**
mad maddie:	**i text lots of ppl, zoe**
mad maddie:	**jana especially liked the endorsements section, where he gives his lubricant rec in 12 tasty flavors.**
zoegirl:	yes, well, that's enough fun and games for me for today.
mad maddie:	**ur not gonna contact jesus, then? this is a once in a lifetime opportunity!!!**

SnowAngel: hola, maddie. u said u had an idea for our halloween costumes?

mad maddie: **yeah, how about we go as fungus, mold, and dust?**

SnowAngel: *wrinkles nose*

mad maddie: **c'mon, it would be great. we could get some cotton batting and spray paint it a nasty green color, then glue it on garbage bags or something.**

SnowAngel: 😖

mad maddie: **do u have a better plan? u've trashed all my other suggestions.**

SnowAngel: i still think the three little pigs would be adorable.

mad maddie: **only i don't do adorable. so what do u say— fungus, mold, and dust?**

SnowAngel: hmm. if i was dust, i could be a dust bunny. that cld be cute.

mad maddie: **i wanna be fungus, so i can say "there's a fungus among us."**

SnowAngel: i'm NOT gonna look all gross, tho. i'll wear a gray leotard and pin on a fluffy tail, and i'll glue some ears to a headband.

mad maddie: **snazz yourself up however u want. i'll be the one in a garbage bag.**

SnowAngel: then it's settled. i'll call zoe and tell her she's mold. 🙂

mad maddie: **tell me the truth: do i have a "mean" look?**

SnowAngel: what, other than your regular expression?

mad maddie: **ha ha**

mad maddie: **wait—r u serious?**

SnowAngel: first tell me what ur talking about. who said u have a mean look?

mad maddie:	my cousin lily. i'm at my aunt's house right now, and during dinner lily said i gave her a mean look. she'd said something about wanting to be a hairdresser when she gets older, and in my mind i rolled my eyes. BUT THAT'S ALL.
SnowAngel:	what's so bad about wanting to be a hairdresser?
mad maddie:	nothing, i guess. it's just such a girlie thing to wanna be. i want lily to grow up tough and fiesty.
SnowAngel:	like u?
mad maddie:	she's only 10—she shouldn't dream of doing ppl's hair. anywayz, she said i give mean looks all the time. do i?!!
SnowAngel:	*ponders*
mad maddie:	u have to THINK about it?
SnowAngel:	well, u do have this disdainful air about u sometimes, like everyone's really dumb except u. and u have this way of cutting your eyes at someone that can make her kinda shrivel up.
SnowAngel:	it's not a BAD thing, necessarily.
mad maddie:	oh, great
SnowAngel:	u've given it to me a couple of times, your mean look.
mad maddie:	like when?
SnowAngel:	like today during our free period when i happened to mention to jana that u have a boyfriend.
mad maddie:	i did not
SnowAngel:	u made me wanna crawl up and die.
mad maddie:	but that's cuz u gave jana misinformation.
mad maddie:	ian's not technically my "boyfriend." it sounds so so teeny-bopper-ish when u put it like that.
SnowAngel:	whatever
SnowAngel:	hey, do *i* have a mean look?
mad maddie:	u?!!
SnowAngel:	yes, me. is that so impossible?

mad maddie: u do not have a mean look, angela. sorry to disappoint u.

SnowAngel: oh, what do u know. i bet i DO have a mean look. i bet it makes ppl quake in their boots.

mad maddie: if by "ppl" u mean "little baby kittens," then maybe. before they wobble over and lick your face.

SnowAngel: *shoots daggers with eyes*

mad maddie: aw, look at all the baby kittens coming over! they're so sweet!

SnowAngel: 👿

SnowAngel: r we still on for tomorrow night?

mad maddie: i told ian we'd meet at 7:00 at zoe's house, since she lives in the ritziest neighborhood. we're talking full-size snickers, baby. none of that "fun size" malarkey for OUR healthy appetites.

Sun, Oct 31, 5:45 PM E.D.T.

SnowAngel: BOO!

zoegirl: hey, angela. and boo to you too.

SnowAngel: got yr costume ready for tonight?

zoegirl: pretty much. you?

SnowAngel: yep. i ended up making my bunny fur out of dryer lint (since i'm a DUST bunny, get it?), which i glued strategically over my leotard. *wiggles fanny suggestively*

zoegirl: only you would find a way to sex up a dust bunny.

SnowAngel: me, to gorgeous trick-or-treater: "hey there, big boy. want me to nibble your carrot?"

zoegirl: me, to gorgeous trick-or-treater: "hey there, big boy. want me to give you jock itch?"

zoegirl: because i'm MOLD, get it? you and maddie made me be mold.

SnowAngel: "mold" doesn't offer as many opportunities for

	seduction, that's true. however, perhaps if u offered to itch his jock . . .
zoegirl:	i'll pass
SnowAngel:	hey, doug called about an hour ago, and i kinda invited him to come trick-or-treating with us. steve too. do you care?
zoegirl:	is doug the gorgeous trick-or-treater whose carrot you want to nibble? 🥕
SnowAngel:	NO! god, no. it's just that he asked if i wanted to go to a party with him, and i turned him down since i already had plans with y'all. so then i asked him if HE wanted to join US, totally expecting him to decline. only he didn't.
zoegirl:	i'm just teasing u, angela. i don't care if they come.
SnowAngel:	they're, uh, dressing up as star trek characters.
zoegirl:	why does that not surprise me?
SnowAngel:	maddie better not make fun of them. i called to warn her, but she didn't answer.
zoegirl:	if she gets here before you do, i'll tell her.

Sun, Oct 31, 7:25 PM E.D.T.

| SnowAngel: | maddieeeeee! where u be? |

Sun, Oct 31, 8:13 PM E.D.T.

| SnowAngel: | seriously, mads. everyone's waiting. |
| SnowAngel: | mads??? |

Sun, Oct 31, 8:30 PM E.D.T.

| SnowAngel: | all right, we're leaving since prime trick-or-treating time ends when all the little kids have to stop and go to bed. text me. i'll tell u where we r so u can meet up with us! |

mad maddie: angela? u awake?

SnowAngel: wtf, maddie? it's one in the morning! WHERE THE HELL WERE U TONIGHT?!!

mad maddie: thank god ur awake. oh, praise jesus, thank god!

SnowAngel: yeah, cuz i've been sitting here WORRYING about you. i called you three different times and you never answered. plus all those texts. i was afraid u'd gotten into an accident or something!

mad maddie: i didn't, so relax, ok?

mad maddie: whoa. i can hardly keep my ffinre on the keys.

SnowAngel: your what?

mad maddie: my fingers. that's what i mean

mad maddie: god, they're fat

SnowAngel: your fingers? what r u talking about?

mad maddie: i hate myself. i know u do too. eveyroen does, so u can just admit it.

SnowAngel: maddie, what is going on? ur acting REALLY weird.

mad maddie: well, u would be 2 if u were me. whihc u should be glad ur not, and i'm so not kidding.

mad maddie: anyeay, it's not my fault. someone said it was spiekd with everclear. whatever it was, it was nasty, like nasty red kool-aid.

SnowAngel: omg. r u DRUNK?

mad maddie: i had three galsess. it was nasty.

SnowAngel: where the hell were u that u were drinking everclear punch? and why was that so much more important than hanging out with us like u'd promised? i showed up, zoe showed up, doug and steve showed up, even ian showed up.

SnowAngel: where WERE u?

mad maddie: don't be mean to me, ok?

mad maddie: sonething bad happened

SnowAngel: what do u mean?

SnowAngel:	shit. WERE u in an accident?
mad maddie:	i went to a party with jana. it was at her brother's frat house.
SnowAngel:	WHAT?!! U BLEW US OFF FOR JANA?!!
mad maddie:	and there was punch, and jana was being really funny and mkating me drink it, but really i think she was mad at me cuz
mad maddie:	nvm
SnowAngel:	cuz what?
mad maddie:	cuz of something i said which was a joke but she got mad anyway. and then i must have really been out of it cuz i ended up dancing on this table and jana was laughing and i wsa laughing only now i don't think it was so hilarius.
mad maddie:	cuz, angela?
SnowAngel:	what happened, mads?
mad maddie:	my shirt says "x-men two, the time has come."
SnowAngel:	x-men?
SnowAngel:	u don't have an x-men shirt
SnowAngel:	u wouldn't be caught dead in an x-men shirt.
mad maddie:	i know
SnowAngel:	so where's YOUR shirt?
mad maddie:	gone, i guess, cuz i'm sure as hell not going back to the frat house to get it.
SnowAngel:	yr shirt is at the frat house?
mad maddie:	and my bra. adios! sayonara!
SnowAngel:	wait a minute. are u saying what i think ur saying? did u, like, take your shirt off on purpose? AND your bra?
mad maddie:	ppl threw money at me, angela. i remember ppl thwoing, like, dimes and quarters and shit.
SnowAngel:	holy fuck
SnowAngel:	where was jana during all of this? why didn't she do something to stop it?

mad maddie: gee, i dunno, cuz i was embarraasing the hell out of her? she must HATE me now.

SnowAngel: no. this makes no sense.

SnowAngel: why didn't she just pull u away? or get u to go to the bathroom with her or something?

mad maddie: she was drunk too. it wasn't her fault.

SnowAngel: u sure? cuz i'm thinking about what u said, about how she was mad at u. and i'm thinking that it sounds incredibly unlikely that she was just, like, an innocent bystander in all this.

mad maddie: ???

mad maddie: no understand.

mad maddie: i thought talking to u would make me feel bettre, but it's just mkaing me feel worse.

SnowAngel: maddie, hold on. i'm sorry for making u feel bad, it's just that the whole situation sounds really strange.

mad maddie: AND DON'T TELL ZOE. that's the last thing i need, having her get all holy on me.

SnowAngel: she wouldn't do that.

mad maddie: don't tell. i mean it.

SnowAngel: i won't, i won't. but r u gonna be ok?

SnowAngel: and what about your parents?!! did they freak when u came in?

mad maddie: they're at some paarty. i'm all alone.

SnowAngel: at least u didn't get busted. THAT'S good.

mad maddie: whoopee

SnowAngel: ur worrying me, maddie. do u want me to come over?

mad maddie: how wld u do that?

SnowAngel: i dunno. i'd find a way.

mad maddie: thx, but no thx

SnowAngel: r u sure?

mad maddie: i'm positive. i just wannt go to bed.

SnowAngel: all right, well, we'll talk more tomorrow.

mad maddie:	whatevs
SnowAngel:	*hug hug hug* good night! i luv u! EVERYTHING'S GONNA BE OK!!!

Mon, Nov 1, 6:21 PM E.D.T.

zoegirl:	hey there, mads. how are you doing?
mad maddie:	if ur txting just to yell at me some more, i don't wanna hear it.
zoegirl:	what? i never yelled at u.
mad maddie:	in homeroom u did. maybe u didn't yell, but close enough.
zoegirl:	because i was mad that you blew us off. but now i'm just worried about you. you seemed so down today.
mad maddie:	whatevs
zoegirl:	is something going on? did something happen at that stupid frat party?
mad maddie:	no. god.
zoegirl:	then why are you acting this way?
zoegirl:	if anyone has the right to be upset, it's me and angela, not you.
mad maddie:	oh, now that's supportive. if something HAD happened, i'd really wanna tell u now.
zoegirl:	so something DID happen! i saw u talking to jana at lunch, and she didn't look happy either. did you two have a fight?
mad maddie:	what do u mean she didn't look happy?
zoegirl:	i don't know. she looked like she didn't want to be there. she kept glancing around like she was really bored.
mad maddie:	she was distracted. she had to find terri to get the english assignment.
zoegirl:	if you say so

mad maddie:	ppl do get distracted, zoe. not everybody is as perfect as u r.
zoegirl:	ok, fine
mad maddie:	u act like u don't believe me. why? is there something ur not telling me?
zoegirl:	hey, i've told u everything i know, which is nothing. is there something YOU'RE not telling ME?
zoegirl:	well, is there???
mad maddie:	i don't want you flipping out.
zoegirl:	i'm your FRIEND. just tell me.
mad maddie:	maybe we r having a fight, me and jana. i dunno. it's all so screwed up.
zoegirl:	did she do something?
mad maddie:	u said u weren't gonna flip out!
zoegirl:	what, i can't even ask questions?
mad maddie:	this is exactly why i didn't wanna talk to u!
zoegirl:	just tell me what's going on!!!
mad maddie:	fine. yes, jana's pissed at me, which i totally don't get. i had a few cups of punch, that's all. anywayz, so did she. and the punch was spiked, apparently.
zoegirl:	wait—did you get drunk? as in, DRUNK drunk?
zoegirl:	i thought you knew better than that.
mad maddie:	oh, that's great. what are you saying, like father like daughter?
zoegirl:	NO! i didn't mean it like that, i swear.
zoegirl:	but is that why jana got mad?
mad maddie:	no
zoegirl:	then WHY?
mad maddie:	cuz according to her, i made her look bad.
zoegirl:	what?! how?
mad maddie:	she said i was out of control and that i made a complete fool out of myself. but SHE was the one

	egging me on the whole time! anywayz, i don't think it's really about that.
zoegirl:	egging you on to do what, drink the punch?
mad maddie:	i think it's about something i said earlier that afternoon.
mad maddie:	she called and asked if i could give her a ride to her brother's frat house, and i said sure. so i drove over and picked her up, and as we were driving to georgia tech, she told me this really funny story about terri.
zoegirl:	what was the story?
mad maddie:	well, terri has this thing about other ppl's spit, right? and she never wants to share her food or her water bottle or anything. she's totally anal about it. so at lunch on friday when terri got up to get a napkin, jana took terri's fork and licked it. then everyone else at the table licked it too.
mad maddie:	jana waited till terri came back and started eating, and then she told her what they'd done. isn't that hysterical?
zoegirl:	no, it's mean and it's disgusting. what did terri do?
mad maddie:	she freaked, obviously. and she must have really cussed jana out, cuz in the car jana was talking about what a bitch terri was for getting so bent out of shape.
mad maddie:	and i guess i said, "oh, like u wouldn't? what about when margaret called u a lesbo?"
zoegirl:	margaret called jana a lesbo? such a dumb word. such a STUPID word.
mad maddie:	apparently it was after PE one day last week. i wasn't there, i just heard about it.
mad maddie:	jana was strutting around in the locker room, and i guess she was naked, and margaret asked if she

was a lesbo. supposedly she did it in this super-concerned way, like, "it's ok, u can tell US," and it made everyone crack up.

zoegirl: so now we know they're homophobic jerks, maddie . . .

mad maddie: but when i brought it up in the car, i was completely joking. i was just teasing her, like how u and me and angela do with each other.

zoegirl: what did jana say?

mad maddie: her face got hard and she said, "oh, sweet, coming from u. ur the biggest lesbo around, always staring at me and laughing at everything i say!"

zoegirl: okay, what you're telling me is wrong in so many different ways. you know that, right?

mad maddie: i know. i was like, SHIT.

mad maddie: so i totally backed off, and time passed and i thought everything was ok.

mad maddie: i mean, i went inside with her when we got to her brother's frat house, and it seemed like things were fine b/w us. she kept introducing me to ppl and getting me to help pick music and stuff.

zoegirl: did you forget that you were supposed to be meeting us?

mad maddie: no! at eight i was like, "i have GOT to go," but jana said, "stay." and i was afraid she'd get pissed again if i didn't. and then she said, "yr friends have probably left by now anyway."

zoegirl: we hadn't. we waited until 8:30. we waited for YOU, maddie.

mad maddie: i SAID i was sorry. anyway, the party didn't even turn out to be fun, so u can be happy about that. in fact, it was worse than un-fun.

zoegirl: what do you mean?

mad maddie: god. i just wish jana would start acting normal

	again, cuz she, like, wouldn't even talk to me in study hall. is it really over that stupid lesbo remark?
zoegirl:	jana's a bitch, maddie. and you know i don't use that word.
mad maddie:	whatevs
mad maddie:	so . . . angela said ian showed up at your house. was he mad?
zoegirl:	that you weren't there? more like hurt, i'd say.
mad maddie:	shit
zoegirl:	he kept
zoegirl:	never mind
mad maddie:	what?
zoegirl:	he kept asking questions, like "do you think she's ok? do you think she got lost?" like there's any way you could get lost driving to my house.
mad maddie:	shit
zoegirl:	don't worry. you can call and straighten things out.
mad maddie:	no thx, i'll just wait till i see him. i don't think i can handle another guilt trip right now.
mad maddie:	god, this sucks
zoegirl:	look, maddie. it's over. ian will understand when u explain what happened.
zoegirl:	as for jana, i don't like any of it.
zoegirl:	i know you're upset, but maybe it's for the best. maybe it just goes to show what kind of friend she really is.
mad maddie:	cld she really hate me so much that she wouldn't want to be my friend anymore?
mad maddie:	no. i'm overreacting. she'll come around.
mad maddie:	anywayz, DON'T tell angela any of what i told u. i don't want the two of u talking about this behind my back.
zoegirl:	maddie! we would never do that.

mad maddie: still, i want you to promise.

zoegirl: i promise, i promise

mad maddie: cuz like u said, it's over. and now i'm gonna go crash, maybe take a nap.

zoegirl: be easy on yourself!

Mon, Nov 1, 8:02 PM E.D.T.

SnowAngel: something is clearly wrong if i'm at the mall and i can't even find the enthusiasm to go to victoria's secret, right?

zoegirl: for you to pass up victoria's secret? yes, something is wrong.

zoegirl: what's going on? is it about maddie? are you worried about her too?

SnowAngel: i called her from the gap and told her the pastel sweater sets were on sale, and she didn't even snort.

zoegirl: ooo, that's bad

SnowAngel: so now i'm sitting by the fountain staring at all the pennies in the water. all the lost wishes.

SnowAngel: it's very depressing, zoe

zoegirl: (((((((((hugs)))))))))

SnowAngel: did maddie tell u anything about what happened? u know, at that frat party?

zoegirl: uh, not really. just that she didn't have fun. did she tell you anything when you talked to her just now?

SnowAngel: the same thing

zoegirl: huh. well, she'll snap out of it. she'll be okay.

SnowAngel: i guess. only . . . i kinda think there's more going on than she's admitting.

zoegirl: what do you mean?

SnowAngel: well, u didn't hear it from me, but i think something happened b/w her and jana.

zoegirl:	so she DID tell you!
SnowAngel:	tell me what?
zoegirl:	about how maddie called jana a . . . a mean word for a lesbian . . . but only because margaret called her that first.
SnowAngel:	what's a mean word for a lesbian? i'm confused.
zoegirl:	starts with L, ends with O . . .
SnowAngel:	lesbo. right. hate that word.
zoegirl:	and that's what maddie and jana had that big fight about. isn't that what you're talking about? and then after that maddie got wasted and made a fool out of herself?
SnowAngel:	omg, she told me not to tell you!
zoegirl:	she told *me* not to tell *you*!
SnowAngel:	that is sooooo maddie. i can't believe this!
SnowAngel:	except i hadn't heard about the lesbian remark, which throws a new spin on things.
zoegirl:	it does?
SnowAngel:	i'm talking about the whole shirt thing. cuz if jana wanted to get back at maddie, u'd think she'd do something that didn't involve, like, a girl doing a striptease. cuz what does THAT say about jana, u know?
zoegirl:	HUH?
SnowAngel:	don't make me say it. it's too embarrassing. and for everyone to be throwing money? i know maddie was drunk, and i'm not BLAMING her, but god.
zoegirl:	angela, what are you talking about?
SnowAngel:	wait . . . u said she told u!
zoegirl:	i'm beginning to think she left some parts out.
SnowAngel:	*gulps* uh . . .
zoegirl:	you have to tell me, angela. you started it, and you have to finish it. WHAT HAPPENED?
SnowAngel:	shit

SnowAngel:	well, maddie got drunk on kool-aid punch, right?
zoegirl:	yes. i know that part.
SnowAngel:	she didn't exactly explain it, but i get the sense that jana got her to do, like, a table dance in front of the whole party.
zoegirl:	no way. that's impossible.
SnowAngel:	she ended up with somebody else's shirt on, zo. and no bra.
zoegirl:	oh god.
zoegirl:	oh my god.
zoegirl:	all she told me was that she'd gotten a little out of control.
SnowAngel:	that's one way to put it
zoegirl:	CRAP, angela
SnowAngel:	i know
zoegirl:	this is terrible. i can't even get my head around it. she took her SHIRT off?
SnowAngel:	but listen, we've got to be super careful not to let on that we talked. she'd be furious if she knew.
zoegirl:	uh, YEAH. i think we should pretty much not bring the party up at all, but if SHE wants to talk about it, she can.
SnowAngel:	mainly we'll just act normal, altho we'll be extra extra nice to her.
zoegirl:	sounds good
zoegirl:	still, angela.
zoegirl:	god.

Mon, Nov 1, 8:21 PM E.D.T.

SnowAngel:	it's strange that maddie hates how much her dad drinks . . . but then she goes out and does the same thing. it's strange, isn't it?
zoegirl:	i know. i thought of that too.
SnowAngel:	poor maddie!!!

zoegirl:	want to hear something gross?
mad maddie:	**i guess**
zoegirl:	i ran into megan at eckerd's, and she was buying one of those long wraparound bandages for her two-year-old brother. apparently he fell off a chair, only the chair fell with him, and it landed on his hands and peeled three of his fingernails off. isn't that awful?
mad maddie:	**oh, ick**
zoegirl:	i know. they have to keep his hand wrapped up for like a week, which is why megan was buying more bandages.
zoegirl:	she said his fingers look all sad and raw, like little sea creatures without their shells.
mad maddie:	**poor kid. that sucks.**
zoegirl:	yeah
zoegirl:	that's all i have to say, really. i just wanted to shoot the breeze.
mad maddie:	**shoot away**
zoegirl:	i already did
mad maddie:	**oh**
zoegirl:	so . . . i guess i'll go to bed.
zoegirl:	unless you have anything you want to talk about?
mad maddie:	**nope, not really**
zoegirl:	that's ok. you're doing all right, though?
mad maddie:	**hmm, let's think. jana's still acting as if i no longer exist, terri and margaret whisper to each other every time they see me, and i still haven't gotten up the nerve to call ian.**
mad maddie:	**ohhhh, and you and angela r walking on eggshells around me cuz u think i'm gonna collapse. so yes, i'm absolutely fabulous. thx for asking.**
zoegirl:	i'm sorry. i didn't mean to make things worse.

zoegirl:	is there anything i can do?
mad maddie:	yeah, go to bed and stop worrying about me. it makes me feel pathetic.
zoegirl:	you're not pathetic, maddie.
mad maddie:	whatevs. night, zo.
zoegirl:	uh, ok. good night.

Wed, Nov 3, 8:21 PM E.D.T.

SnowAngel:	mad-a-lad-a-ding-dong!
mad maddie:	ouch. tone down the enthusiasm, i beg u.
SnowAngel:	where'd u disappear to after math?
mad maddie:	nowhere, i just went home.
SnowAngel:	but i thought we were going out for ice cream! 🍦
mad maddie:	u had a drama club meeting, remember?
SnowAngel:	u could have waited for me. it only lasted an hour.
mad maddie:	i felt like going home, that's all.
SnowAngel:	well. let's go now. *bats eyelashes adorably*
mad maddie:	no thanks
SnowAngel:	why not?
mad maddie:	i'm not in the mood.
SnowAngel:	how can u not be in the mood for ice cream? c'mon, sling yourself into the gremlin and come pick me up.
mad maddie:	sorry
SnowAngel:	pralines 'n' cream, mint chocolate chip, chocolate mousse . . .
mad maddie:	i said no, angela. give it up.
SnowAngel:	u can't stay holed up forever, u know.
mad maddie:	oh god, here it comes
SnowAngel:	it's true! u've got to show jana that maybe she thinks she can drop friends whenever she wants to, but that *you're* sticking with us, baby. u don't need a friend who calls her other friends "lesbos," anyway.

SnowAngel:	be strong. show her that you cldn't care less what she thinks of u.
mad maddie:	**that's a great plan. only i DO care.**
SnowAngel:	but why?
mad maddie:	**wait. who told u about margaret calling jana a lesbo?**
SnowAngel:	u did
mad maddie:	**no, i didn't**
SnowAngel:	obviously u did, or how would i know?
mad maddie:	**fuck**
mad maddie:	**did u talk to zoe? don't lie!**
SnowAngel:	what r u talking about? of course i talked to zoe. i talk to zoe every day.
mad maddie:	**u know what i mean. did u talk to zoe about . . . that night?**
SnowAngel:	no!
mad maddie:	**did u?**
SnowAngel:	NO, i swear!
mad maddie:	**ANGELA!**
SnowAngel:	if i tell u, will u promise not to be mad?
mad maddie:	**omg! i can't believe u!**
mad maddie:	**PLEASE tell me u didn't tell her about the x-men shirt. PLEASE.**
SnowAngel:	she said u'd told her! i thought she already knew! it's yr fault for telling us each a little bit and then expecting us not to worry about u!
mad maddie:	**i hate u, angela. i really do.**
SnowAngel:	don't say that. it was totally an accident, ok? i'm sorry!!!
mad maddie:	**FUCK. did u tell her everything?**
SnowAngel:	not EVERYTHING, just . . . everything u'd told me. but come on, we're talking about zoe. she doesn't care!
mad maddie:	**FUCK.**

mad maddie:	**zoe is the last person on earth i wanted to know about this. she already has so many things to feel superior to me about. now she thinks i'm a slut too.**
SnowAngel:	ur not a slut
mad maddie:	**yeah, just like ur not a lying bitch.**
SnowAngel:	maddie!
mad maddie:	**fuck off, angela. go sob to zoe about it and STAY OUT OF MY FUCKING BUSINESS!!!**

Wed, Nov 3, 8:59 PM E.D.T.

SnowAngel:	shit, zoe. shit, shit, shit.
zoegirl:	angela, what's wrong?
SnowAngel:	it slipped out. maddie and i were txting, and it just slipped out.
zoegirl:	what slipped out?
zoegirl:	oh, crap—about the frat party? or rather, the fact that you told me about the frat party?
SnowAngel:	she's pissed. she called me a bitch.
zoegirl:	what?!
SnowAngel:	which pisses ME off, but more than that i just feel bad. i didn't mean to make her so upset!
SnowAngel:	oh god, i think i'm gonna throw up.
zoegirl:	angela, relax. it's going to be okay. somehow it's going to be okay.
SnowAngel:	i dunno, zoe. she is PISSED.
zoegirl:	should i call her?
SnowAngel:	not unless u want her to bite your head off.
zoegirl:	it's just, you shouldn't be the only one she's mad at. we both messed up, not just you.
SnowAngel:	well, thx for saying that.
zoegirl:	does she know that we weren't gossiping about her? that we were just worried? i mean, she kind of brought this on herself.

SnowAngel:	i told her that. didn't go over so well.
zoegirl:	oh
SnowAngel:	*breathe, angela, breathe*
zoegirl:	she was that mad, huh?
SnowAngel:	u wldn't believe
zoegirl:	well, tomorrow we'll be all humble and apologetic. she'll calm down. by lunch everything will be back to normal.
SnowAngel:	ur right. i hope. cuz what else is she gonna do, give us the silent treatment?
zoegirl:	she's maddie. we'll work this out.
SnowAngel:	okay. but . . . u don't think i'm a horrible person?
zoegirl:	you're not a horrible person, i promise.

Thu, Nov 4, 5:38 PM E.D.T.

zoegirl:	hi, maddie.
mad maddie:	**screw u**
zoegirl:	seriously?
zoegirl:	maddie, come on. you wouldn't answer your phone and TALK TO ME, but you're fine with texting me and being a jerk?
mad maddie:	**yep, that's me, the jerk. thanks for rubbing it in.**
zoegirl:	quit being this way. you wouldn't talk to me in homeroom—thanks a lot, that made me feel terrific—and who knows where you were at lunch. don't you even want to hear what i have to say?
mad maddie:	**rent a billboard. then the whole world will know.**
zoegirl:	look, i'm sorry. i've told you 100 times. i'm trying to be patient, but this is getting ridiculous.
mad maddie:	**ooo, i'm scared! r u gonna quote the scriptures at me? drag me to church? if i did a striptease in front of a teacher instead of in front of ten million frat boys, would THAT be ok?**
zoegirl:	again, I AM SORRY you are sad. I AM SORRY i'm

	part of what made you sad. but i'm not gonna talk to you if you're going to be like this.
mad maddie:	a) "sad" doesn't even begin to cover it, and b) u say u wanna "talk," but only on your terms.
mad maddie:	well here's a news flash: i don't give a rat's ass. so forget about me and go spin your little fantasies about mr. h, since that's all u ever do anywayz. at least i'm not a stuck-up prude afraid to actually have fun.
zoegirl:	you're not being fair, maddie. and you're being . . . mean.
mad maddie:	yeah? tell it to angela. u 2 can cry on each other's shoulders and slam me behind my back.
mad maddie:	oh. wait. u've already done that, haven't u?
zoegirl:	that's it. i'm done.
mad maddie:	boo-fucking-hoo. and in case u missed it the first time around, SCREW U!

	Thu, Nov 4, 8:01 PM E.D.T.
SnowAngel:	saw maddie's pissy tweet. lemme guess: u txted her?
zoegirl:	i did, and i tried so hard to actually *talk* to her.
zoegirl:	it was a disaster. she wldn't listen at all.
SnowAngel:	tell me about it. she's been horrible all day.
zoegirl:	in homeroom, she stalked away right in the middle of my sentence. kristin was like, "what was that all about?" and i couldn't even tell her.
SnowAngel:	i feel bad for her . . . but she's being a baby.
zoegirl:	it's like she's not even the same maddie.
SnowAngel:	i know
zoegirl:	so what should we do?
SnowAngel:	give her time, i guess. what else can we do?
zoegirl:	i don't know
SnowAngel:	she'll come around. she has to.

SnowAngel:	so tomorrow's friday. u going to friday morning fellowship?
zoegirl:	yeah. i'm, uh, actually leading the prayer. it'll be my first time.
SnowAngel:	that's great. good luck.
zoegirl:	thanks. and thanks for not making fun of me.
SnowAngel:	of course 😇
SnowAngel:	u know what u shld do while yr there? say a prayer for maddie too!

Fri, Nov 5, 6:45 PM E.D.T.

SnowAngel:	hey, mads. r u done being a drama queen yet?
SnowAngel:	maddie, come on. i know ur there.
SnowAngel:	fine. u know where i am.

Fri, Nov 5, 7:12 PM E.D.T.

zoegirl:	maddie, it's me
zoegirl:	well, der. you obviously know that. i'm at java joe's, and i'm thinking of you, and MISSING you.
zoegirl:	maddie, plz. you've at least got to talk to us.
zoegirl:	maddie?
zoegirl:	please please please call me when ur ready to talk!

Fri, Nov 5, 7:20 PM E.D.T.

zoegirl:	maddie's still not talking to me.
SnowAngel:	i know. me neither.
zoegirl:	seriously, she didn't say one word to me at school.
SnowAngel:	it's ridiculous. mr. miklos had her pass out the quizzes in geometry, and she slapped one on my desk without even looking at me.
zoegirl:	i want to shake her and tell her how stupid she's being. i want to shake her AND hug her.
SnowAngel:	me too. but now she's got her jana friends, so maybe she doesn't need us anymore.

zoegirl:	except jana's cold-shouldering her just like she's cold-shouldering us. haven't you noticed?
SnowAngel:	really? ha. that's kinda funny—only it's not, is it?
zoegirl:	which is why it's doubly stupid that she's turning her back on us.
zoegirl:	we wouldn't judge her like jana is.
SnowAngel:	she's just being stubborn
SnowAngel:	r u still coming over tonight?
zoegirl:	yeah. my mom's going to drop me off as soon as she's done getting ready for her business dinner.
SnowAngel:	👍
zoegirl:	but . . . what should we do about maddie?
SnowAngel:	i'll try txting one more time. if she doesn't answer then it's her own fault.

Fri, Nov 5, 7:39 PM E.D.T.

SnowAngel:	hi, madigan. i know yr there, so u might as well answer.
SnowAngel:	*shakes maddie like a rag doll* ANSWER ME!!!
SnowAngel:	this is getting soooooooooo old. u realize that, right?
SnowAngel:	well, zoe's coming over to spend the night, and we want u to come too, even if all u do is sit there like a bump on a log. so drive over if u want, ok?
SnowAngel:	*makes megaphone with hands* M-A-D-D-I-E!!!!!
SnowAngel:	all right 😟
SnowAngel:	u know where to find us!

Sun, Nov 7, 1:45 PM E.S.T.

zoegirl:	any word from maddie ?
SnowAngel:	and . . . the answer is still no. no word from maddie. nada, zilch, zero words from maddie.
zoegirl:	i thought maybe she'd call, since she worked with ian last night. as far as i know that's the first time she's seen him since halloween.

SnowAngel:	yeah, i wonder how that went. i wonder if she was as weird with him as she is with us.
zoegirl:	who knows
SnowAngel:	how was it, going to church with mr. h this morning??? ⛪
zoegirl:	it was good
SnowAngel:	good? that's all ur gonna say?
zoegirl:	hmm. i guess i feel strange talking about other stuff with this whole maddie mess going on.
SnowAngel:	why? we DO have lives apart from her, u know.
zoegirl:	true
SnowAngel:	so tell me! did mr. h finally kiss u? *smooch, smooch*
zoegirl:	yeah, right there at the altar, in front of God and everybody.
SnowAngel:	REALLY?
zoegirl:	angela!
SnowAngel:	well, did u have any romantic moments? meaningful glances, knee-touches, that sort of thing?
zoegirl:	the car ride was nice, even though we just talked about school. it's so bizarre. it's like there we are, alone in his car with all of this . . . energy . . . bouncing around between us, and what do we do? we talk about english and the shakespeare festival and who our favorite authors are.
SnowAngel:	*winks lasciviously* verbal foreplay
zoegirl:	i don't think so
zoegirl:	only . . .
SnowAngel:	what?
zoegirl:	he did mention that he's house-sitting for greg kravitz's parents beginning on the 17th. and he also mentioned that the house has an outdoor hot tub.
SnowAngel:	omg. AND?

zoegirl:	and he kind of hinted around that maybe i could come over one night. that we could, um, gaze at the stars.
SnowAngel:	IN the hot tub?! IN your bathing suits?! OR— *gasp!*—MAYBE IN YOUR NUDIE PANTS!!!!
zoegirl:	angela, stop! 🍪
zoegirl:	we will not be in our "nudie pants." omigosh. he hasn't even technically invited me!
SnowAngel:	when he does, will u say yes?
zoegirl:	i don't know. it makes me nervous just thinking about it.
SnowAngel:	good nervous or bad nervous?
zoegirl:	i don't know!
zoegirl:	ack. can we talk about something else, please?
SnowAngel:	sure. have u picked which swimsuit ur gonna wear? 👀
zoegirl:	😡!!!!
SnowAngel:	not yr blue one-piece. it comes up to, like, your collarbone. and not that nasty red one with the worn spots in the butt . . . altho i suppose that *cld* work to your advantage. 🙂
zoegirl:	enough
SnowAngel:	you'll have to borrow my bikini with the orange flowery bits on it, that's all there is to it. and u should probably go to a tanning salon. otherwise u'll look like a dead codfish, no offense.
zoegirl:	if i wore your bikini, it would fall right off me. (and stop right there with what you're thinking!) and i'm not going to a tanning salon. i am morally opposed to tanning salons.
SnowAngel:	hey, u asked for my advice
zoegirl:	no, i didn't
SnowAngel:	well u shld have
zoegirl:	am i really too pale to wear a bathing suit?

SnowAngel:	it's november—of course ur pale. i am too, altho it hardly matters since i'm not going hot-tubbing with my lusty young buck of an english teacher.
zoegirl:	😦
zoegirl:	i think i'm gonna faint.
SnowAngel:	u can always use tanning creme if u don't wanna go to a tanning booth. or tanning foam. they even make tanning wipes now, like baby wipes, only not just for yr lady parts.
SnowAngel:	(in fact, not really for yr lady parts at all . . .)
SnowAngel:	(unless u want a tan va-jay-jay???)
zoegirl:	and now i'm going to go.
SnowAngel:	but we haven't discussed yr thong possibilities! yikes, u better start doing your butt exercises. *and squeeze and lift and squeeze and lift and pump and pump and pump!* 😀

Mon, Nov 8, 9:21 PM E.S.T.

SnowAngel:	this is getting to be a very sad pattern, but: any luck with maddie today?
zoegirl:	no, you?
SnowAngel:	she shot me a death look when i tried to talk to her in geometry. does that count?
zoegirl:	maddie shoots a good death look, i'll give her that.
SnowAngel:	so, not to be self-absorbed or anything, but does this mean our cumberland island trip is off? thanksgiving's only 2 and a half weeks away.
zoegirl:	i've been wondering about that too. maddie was so psyched about it.
SnowAngel:	then she shld get off her high horse and stop being sullen!
SnowAngel:	u know what? i'm gonna text her and ask. even if she doesn't reply, i can at least make her feel guilty about it. it's not fair for her to back out now.

SnowAngel: hey, madikins. it's time to just suck it up and reply, don't you think?

SnowAngel: u know you want to . . .

SnowAngel: fine, i'll talk AT u, then. zoe and i wanna know about our trip to cumberland island. r we still on or not?

SnowAngel: i GUESS we could go even if ur stonewalling us, but what a dreadful car ride. i can see it now: u alone in the front, scowling and clutching the steering wheel, while zoe and i cower in the back, begging u to give us a potty break.

SnowAngel: 💩💩💩

SnowAngel: and our potty needs are even cute, see? 😊

SnowAngel: goddammit, maddie. i hope u don't wait TOO long before talking to us, cuz who knows? we might make other plans!!!!

zoegirl: crap, angela, guess who just called me?

SnowAngel: maddie?!!

zoegirl: i wish!

zoegirl: no, nealie anderson.

SnowAngel: nealie anderson? she says her "s"s weird. why'd she call?

zoegirl: for bad reasons.

zoegirl: nealie's kind of friends with terri springer, and apparently terri just got an awful email from jana. well, nealie thought it was awful. terri thought it was hysterical.

SnowAngel: oh, no

SnowAngel: did it have to do with maddie?

zoegirl: jana sent pictures, angela.

zoegirl: she sent a group email with pics from that frat party, and they were of maddie dancing on the

	table, and angela—she was naked from the waist up!
SnowAngel:	SHIT. someone took pictures?
zoegirl:	apparently, and you know who it was, right? it HAD to be jana!
SnowAngel:	I HATE HER!!!
SnowAngel:	and omg, poor maddie. omg!!!!
zoegirl:	the subject line was "lesbo slut." jana sent it to practically the entire school.
SnowAngel:	shit, shit, SHIT.
SnowAngel:	did U see it? did u ask nealie to forward it to u?
zoegirl:	NO! i don't WANT to see it, angela.
zoegirl:	if it were me? and i knew people were seeing me like that???
SnowAngel:	AAAARRRGH.
SnowAngel:	but why now? why did jana do this NOW, a fucking week later?
zoegirl:	why does jana do ANYTHING she does?
SnowAngel:	so does maddie know?
zoegirl:	i don't know. that's why nealie called me, because she knows maddie's my friend.
SnowAngel:	used to be, at any rate
zoegirl:	you know what i mean. anyway, maddie is still my friend even if i'm no longer hers. maddie will always be my friend.
SnowAngel:	i know. i'm just in shock. i can't believe anyone would do something like that, even jana.
SnowAngel:	should we tell her? maddie, i mean?
zoegirl:	i don't know
SnowAngel:	maybe she won't find out. maybe no one'll mention it.
zoegirl:	yeah, that's likely
SnowAngel:	shld we tell principal russo?
SnowAngel:	or maybe a teacher?

zoegirl:	agh. yes! right?
zoegirl:	but think about how upset maddie got when *you* told *me*. can you imagine her reaction if we brought the grown-ups into it? which would of course involve her parents?
SnowAngel:	i wld NOT want mr. russo seeing pics like that of me. i wld DEFINITELY not want my parents seeing pics like that of me.
zoegirl:	me neither, not in a million years
SnowAngel:	what r we supposed to do, then?
zoegirl:	i have no clue
zoegirl:	maybe we should just stick close tomorrow, so we can be there if someone says something or something bad happens.
SnowAngel:	something *worse*, u mean?
zoegirl:	yeah
SnowAngel:	ok. i feel like that's not enough, but ok.
zoegirl:	we'll know more tomorrow.
zoegirl:	and maybe nealie was wrong and jana only sent it to a few people. not that that's still not awful . . .
SnowAngel:	i hope yr right. crossing my fingers!!!

Tues, Nov 9, 10:09 PM E.S.T.

zoegirl:	maddie?
zoegirl:	are you there?
zoegirl:	just wanted to let u know i'm here. that's all.

Wed, Nov 10, 8:45 PM E.S.T.

SnowAngel:	still no word from maddie, just so u know. not that i shld have expected it, i suppose, but after what happened in geometry, i thought she'd at least want a shoulder to cry on.
zoegirl:	she probably does, but for whatever reason, she doesn't think she can come to us.

SnowAngel:	BUT WE'VE BEEN BEST FRIENDS FOR 4 YEARS!!! who else is she supposed to go to?
zoegirl:	i know, i know
SnowAngel:	it broke my heart to see her striding down the halls with her lips clamped together. it's gotta be killing her. u'd think she'd WANT her friends around her at a time like this, or that she'd at least wanna TALK to us about it!
zoegirl:	maybe it's a pride thing. like, now that everyone knows what happened, she's determined to hold her head up and pretend she doesn't give a damn.
SnowAngel:	tough to do when ppl are interrupting geometry to ask how much she charges for a private party.
zoegirl:	i can't even imagine
SnowAngel:	and what does mr. miklos do? he just stands there blinking and rubbing his neck, saying, "class, class! could we bring it down to a dull roar?"
SnowAngel:	he had no clue, did he?
zoegirl:	do you think *any* of the teachers know?
SnowAngel:	if they did, there'd be a BIG deal being made out of it.
SnowAngel:	*shudders*
zoegirl:	what about maddie's parents. do u think they know?
SnowAngel:	i hope not. i'm sure SHE hasn't told them.
zoegirl:	if it were me, can u imagine what my mom would do?
SnowAngel:	it's lucky mark's out of high school, or he'd have heard about it, and he definitely wld have told them. so MAYBE she's safe.
SnowAngel:	did u see jana after school, sitting on the steps with terri and jane olsen?
zoegirl:	no. what did they do?
SnowAngel:	they were just hanging out, laughing and joking around like "la-di-da, isn't life great."

SnowAngel:	in my head i was like, "u bitch! don't u know that u've ruined someone's life?! don't u even care?"
SnowAngel:	but of course she doesn't, or she wouldn't have sent that email.
zoegirl:	u were right from the beginning, angela. she's evil.
SnowAngel:	one good thing: i was talking to my mom about jana last night—not the specifics of the maddie thing, just in general—and my mom said that girls like jana peak in high school and then wonder why the rest of their lives seem so rotten.
SnowAngel:	so just wait. we'll see jana at our 10th reunion and she'll be fat and pathetic. she'll work at walmart and wear a horrid blue smock.
zoegirl:	maybe
zoegirl:	i almost wish someone would email pics of her doing something embarrassing, you know? maddie made a mistake. maddie did something dumb. yes.
zoegirl:	but jana is no saint. only because she's the kind of person she is, she somehow manages to make everyone else look bad.
SnowAngel:	i'm gonna try maddie again. i know she probably won't talk, but i have to do something!

Wed, Nov 10, 9:15 PM E.S.T.

SnowAngel:	hi, maddie. still not answering my calls, i see. don't u WANT to talk to me?
SnowAngel:	i want to talk to you . . . 😢
SnowAngel:	i just wanted to let u know that i love u. zoe does too. we're still your friends, even if u don't think so. we've always been yr friends, and we always will be.
SnowAngel:	ALWAYS.

Thu, Nov 11, 10:01 PM E.S.T.

SnowAngel: hey, zo. remember in 8th grade when my parents rented a house at myrtle beach, and u and maddie got to stay with us for a whole week? and we had that contest to see who could eat the most banana pudding? 🖐

zoegirl: ha! yes!

zoegirl: and the rule was that the only thing we could wash it down with was fanta grape, and afterward maddie looked pregnant because she'd eaten so much.

zoegirl: what made you think of that?

SnowAngel: nothing, i guess. i was just thinking about all the stuff we've done together.

zoegirl: yeah

zoegirl: i know what u mean

Fri, Nov 12, 5:05 PM E.S.T.

zoegirl: listen, angela . . . i was hoping i could talk to you about something that doesn't have to do with maddie, if that's ok.

SnowAngel: of course. i'm at 7-11 with chrissy, but she can be entertained for a l-o-n-g time in the candy aisle. shoot!

zoegirl: it has to do with mr. h.

SnowAngel: i figured. intrigue!

zoegirl: shut up, it's not THAT exciting. but this morning at friday morning fellowship, he said something that sort of weirded me out.

SnowAngel: were the two of you alone, or were you with the whole group?

zoegirl: the whole group was there, but mr. h and i were sitting at the far end of the table, and no one was paying attention to us.

zoegirl:	at least i don't think anyone was paying attention to us. if they were, and they heard what he said . . .
SnowAngel:	*bams on glass case of hot dogs*
SnowAngel:	what? what did he say?!!
zoegirl:	he was talking about next weekend, which is when he's going to be house-sitting for the kravitzes, and at first it was like . . . sexy. kind of.
zoegirl:	(don't laugh!)
SnowAngel:	what do u mean?
zoegirl:	just that nobody was listening, but they COULD have been. and that made it . . . i don't know. exciting.
SnowAngel:	oh man
zoegirl:	he told me about how nice the kravitzes' house is, and he told me about the hot tub again.
zoegirl:	then he lowered his voice and said, "you're still coming, right?"
SnowAngel:	FUCK.
zoegirl:	please don't say that word. *especially* that word.
SnowAngel:	what'd u say?
zoegirl:	i said, "i think so, yeah," and he said, "good." then he touched my hand really lightly and said, "you can wear your bikini."
SnowAngel:	!!!
SnowAngel:	i was KIDDING when i told u to wear a bikini!
SnowAngel:	i was not . . .
SnowAngel:	u r not . . .
SnowAngel:	TEACHERS ARE NOT SUPPOSED TO SAY "YOU CAN WEAR YOUR BIKINI" TO THEIR STUDENTS!!!!
zoegirl:	i know!
zoegirl:	at first i thought he *was* just teasing me, and i said, "yeah, right, me in a bikini. wouldn't that be a lovely sight."
SnowAngel:	and . . . ?

zoegirl:	and then his eyes kind of dipped over my body, and he said, "it would indeed be a lovely sight. i'm looking forward to it."
SnowAngel:	"it would indeed"?!!
zoegirl:	i know. it sounded fake, like something a cheesy guy on a TV show would say if he was hitting on a girl. although i know how ridiculous that sounds, because why would he hit on me?
SnowAngel:	zoe, u have got to open your eyes. he IS hitting on u. MR. H IS HITTING ON U.
SnowAngel:	the question is, what r u gonna do about it?
zoegirl:	i don't know!
zoegirl:	i'm flattered, i guess. but all of a sudden it feels . . . REAL. in a physical way, like with . . . well, like with *bodies*, and not just as a meeting of the minds.
SnowAngel:	only u would talk about yr affair as a "meeting of the minds."
zoegirl:	NOT an affair.
SnowAngel:	not yet . . .
zoegirl:	anyway, my stomach's in knots, and whenever i think about it, i feel like i'm going to throw up.
SnowAngel:	poor zo. ur just nervous.
zoegirl:	but is that a good thing? should i be nervous, or should i be . . . i don't know . . . suddenly begging to be homeschooled?
SnowAngel:	i can answer that last one. u r *not* allowed to be homeschooled.
zoegirl:	okay. but. i'm 15. he's 24.
zoegirl:	he's 9 years older than me—and he's my teacher.
SnowAngel:	ur just now realizing this?
zoegirl:	no. i'm just now admitting that maybe it's a little sketchy.
SnowAngel:	so ur not gonna go hot-tubbing with him?

zoegirl:	i never said that
SnowAngel:	so u R gonna go hot-tubbing with him?
zoegirl:	i never said that either, although as far as he knows, i am. but if i do, i'm most definitely not wearing a bikini.
SnowAngel:	u should wear one of those granny suits, one of those old-timey ones that covers up your entire body.
SnowAngel:	or a scuba outfit. ha!
zoegirl:	ack, this is not helping
zoegirl:	i wish i could talk to maddie about it, even though i know she'd just make fun of me. but maybe that's what i need.
SnowAngel:	yeah
SnowAngel:	did u hear what happened in 6th period? how brant simms offered her ten bucks for a peep show?
zoegirl:	what an ass
zoegirl:	how'd you hear that?
SnowAngel:	a couple of kids were talking about it in history. they shut up when i sat down.
zoegirl:	poor maddie. poor, poor maddie!!!
SnowAngel:	i saw her walking to her car when i was on my way to drama club. her eyes were all puffy. i called out to her, but of course she didn't turn around.
zoegirl:	she wldn't talk to me when i went up to her during lunch, either.
SnowAngel:	i miss her, zoe 😞
zoegirl:	me too

Sat, Nov 13, 10:30 AM E.S.T.

SnowAngel:	zoe—i have an awesome idea!
zoegirl:	oh yeah?
SnowAngel:	let's make maddie a care package!
zoegirl:	to cheer her up, you mean?

SnowAngel:	exactamundo. we could decorate a box and fill it with candy and tacky magazines and stuff like that.
zoegirl:	hmm . . .
zoegirl:	and we could write her a sappy poem telling her how much we miss her, maybe?
SnowAngel:	perfect
SnowAngel:	altho u'll have to write it since i suck at that stuff.
zoegirl:	maybe we cld take a selfie of the two of us looking sad and forlorn. hey, i know—we cld have our arms over each other's shoulders, and then one of us cld have her other arm out in the air, around the place maddie would be if she were there. it'll show, like, the gap she's left in our friendship. how we aren't whole without her.
SnowAngel:	ooo, ur good. we can send the pic to rite aid and get it printed it up. we can use the quickie service!
zoegirl:	how will we get the care package to her once we've made it? will we actually mail it?
SnowAngel:	nah, we'll just leave it on her doorstep and run.
zoegirl:	i'll c if mom can drop me off. see you soon!

Sat, Nov 13, 6:12 PM E.S.T.

zoegirl:	so how did it go when u dropped off maddie's box? sorry i had to leave so early!
SnowAngel:	at least u got to help me put everything together. oh, and your poem was fabulous. *strikes pose* u r our buddy, our buddy to stay, till ur all dried up and peeled away.
zoegirl:	that part was from an old garfield comic about a dead toad. i can't take credit.
SnowAngel:	who cares, it's funny. and it's perfect for maddie cuz it's mushy but not too mushy. she'll love it.
zoegirl:	did u see her when you delivered it? was she at home?

SnowAngel:	she was, cuz i saw her in the living room, peering at me from behind the curtains. i thought for a minute she was gonna come out, especially when she figured out what i was doing, but she didn't.
zoegirl:	**damn**
SnowAngel:	i even texted her! i was like, "peekaboo! i seeeeeee you!" but she ignored me.
SnowAngel:	but maybe our care package will be just the thing. she can't hold out forever.

Sun, Nov 14, 1:35 PM E.S.T.

SnowAngel:	it's sunday, if you haven't noticed, and, if you haven't noticed, i've been VERY patient, just sitting at Sbux waiting for you to call.
SnowAngel:	but did u call? no. no u did not.
zoegirl:	**what was i supposed to call you about?**
SnowAngel:	r u kidding? TELL ME HOW CHURCH WAS, FOOL!
zoegirl:	**oh, that**
SnowAngel:	did mr. h talk about the hot tub again?
SnowAngel:	did he make any moves when u were in the car together?
zoegirl:	**this time i got my mom to drop me off and pick me up. i thought about riding all that way with him and got freaked out.**
SnowAngel:	why'd u even go, then?
zoegirl:	**well, i do like the church service. i honestly do. and i was worried i'd hurt his feelings if i just didn't show.**
SnowAngel:	huh
SnowAngel:	so did he say anything at all?
zoegirl:	**he told me he liked my dress. he whispered it really softly during one of the hymns.**
SnowAngel:	was he being creepy or cute?
zoegirl:	**i don't know. both?**

zoegirl:	cute, mainly, but i get scared at the thought of being alone with him.
SnowAngel:	uh, zoe? *flicks zoe's head with finger* hate to break it to u, but if ur scared to be alone with a guy, that's called creepy. i think it's time to cut this one loose, soldier.
zoegirl:	what am i supposed to tell him? he bought sparkling apple juice for us and everything!
SnowAngel:	WHAT?!!
zoegirl:	whoops. i wasn't going to mention that.
SnowAngel:	mr. h bought sparkling apple juice? why?
SnowAngel:	OH! for your big hot-tubbing date?!! that is so dorky i think i'm gonna cry. 😢
zoegirl:	he's going to get strawberries and chocolate too, only i'm pretty sure i don't want to go anymore.
zoegirl:	help!
SnowAngel:	this is crazy, zo
zoegirl:	i know
SnowAngel:	want me to call the school board?
zoegirl:	omg, don't even say that. he would be so dead. and so would i!
zoegirl:	anyway, he trusts me. he would freak if he knew i'd told anybody, even you.
SnowAngel:	but c'mon, what is he thinking? that it's normal to be hitting on a 15-year-old student?
zoegirl:	it's my fault for going to backwork all those times. i gave him the wrong idea.
SnowAngel:	u don't seriously believe that, do u?
zoegirl:	kind of
SnowAngel:	first of all, u didn't give him the "wrong" idea, cuz up till now u've totally been crushing on him and u know it.
zoegirl:	i know, which is why i feel so bad.

SnowAngel:	but second of all, HE'S the grown-up. if it's anybody's fault, it's his.
zoegirl:	i don't want it to be anyone's fault. i just want it to be over.
SnowAngel:	so tell him
zoegirl:	what if i'm wrong? what if he just, u know, wants to talk about the Bible?
SnowAngel:	*snorts*
SnowAngel:	in the hot tub while sharing a bottle of sparkling apple juice?
zoegirl:	anyway, everything'll be fine. i'll think of something and it'll all be fine.
SnowAngel:	if u say so
zoegirl:	i've got to go do my homework. but really quickly: any word from maddie?
SnowAngel:	if there was, i would have told u.

Mon, Nov 15, 5:24 PM E.S.T.

SnowAngel:	o. m. g.
SnowAngel:	if i hear one more joke about maddie and the gold club, or maddie charging admission, or maddie being a titty-tease, i'm gonna scream.
zoegirl:	i know!
zoegirl:	and think how awful it must be for maddie. over the weekend she can forget about it (maybe), but then today she had to plod right back to school and deal with it all over again.
SnowAngel:	i'm surprised she came at all. i'd stay at home with a mysterious illness.
zoegirl:	she'd have to face everyone eventually. she couldn't skip forever.
SnowAngel:	i wld. i'd flee to a convent and become a nun.
zoegirl:	you would be a terrible nun.

SnowAngel:	what r u talking about? i look good in black. i'd just have to do away with that headdress thing they wear.
zoegirl:	it's called a wimple
SnowAngel:	god, even the name is dreadful. *pretends to be a nun: excuse me while i put on my pimple—i mean dimple—i mean wimple!*
zoegirl:	don't be a nun, angela.
SnowAngel:	*waves away zoe's foolishness*
SnowAngel:	oh, and u wanna hear something really lovely?
zoegirl:	what?
SnowAngel:	maddie was late to geometry, and there were only two seats left: one next to me and one next to barry beryl. guess which one she picked?
zoegirl:	not barry. really?
SnowAngel:	yes, it's true. she chose barry "the sneeze" beryl over her best friend since 7th grade. namely, me.
zoegirl:	oh, angela. that's so wrong!

Mon, Nov 15, 7:30 PM E.S.T.

SnowAngel:	maddie's not really gonna ditch us forever, right? i mean, deep inside she's still the same maddie, and she knows we're still the same angela and zoe. right?
zoegirl:	i don't know, angela. i thought she would have come around a long time ago.
SnowAngel:	yeah, me too
SnowAngel:	THIS IS SO MESSED UP!!!

Tues, Nov 16, 8:01 PM E.S.T.

SnowAngel:	zoe! BEN SCHLANKER ASKED ME OUT! *squeals and dances about*
zoegirl:	he did? how did THIS happen?

SnowAngel:	today at drama club he made an announcement about a poetry slam at the coffee connection tomorrow night, and he invited us all to come.
zoegirl:	this counts as asking you out?
SnowAngel:	yes, cuz even tho he was talking to the whole room, he looked right at me when he said it. *shakes booty in sexy circles*
zoegirl:	uh, ok
zoegirl:	what's a poetry slam?
SnowAngel:	it's when a bunch of ppl get up and read their poems, and everyone gets a score from 1 to 10. the audience boos or cheers to help the judges decide, and the winner gets, like, fifty dollars and a free pizza.
zoegirl:	is this something you *want* to attend?
SnowAngel:	don't u think it sounds fun?
zoegirl:	actually, yeah. i'm just surprised you do.
SnowAngel:	ye of little faith. i adore poetry.
zoegirl:	mmm-hmm
SnowAngel:	and now we will play pretend, starring moi and ben schlanker.
SnowAngel:	there we r at coffee connection sipping our cappuccinos and having an extremely sophisticated conversation about . . . about . . .
zoegirl:	coffee?
SnowAngel:	about ART. and ben looks into my eyes, which r as blue as a summer sky, and says, "oh, angela, your eyes r as blue as a summer sky."
zoegirl:	ack
SnowAngel:	then he cradles my face in his hand, like he's protecting me from the harsh reality of life, and kisses my eagerly parted lips.
zoegirl:	and the judges raise their cards to show a

	unanimous score of 10! and the coffeehouse goes wild with applause!
SnowAngel:	of course for this fantasy to come true, i first have to decide what to wear.
zoegirl:	how about some clothes?
SnowAngel:	no time for jokes! must go ransack my closet!

Wed, Nov 17, 5:45 PM E.S.T.

SnowAngel:	la la la, la la la, only one more hour till my date with ben!
zoegirl:	so are you texting to describe your lovely, gussied-up self?
SnowAngel:	*clears throat* attire: tight black cords, betty boop t-shirt, black lace-up boots. scent: my mom's "chance" by coco chanel.
zoegirl:	very nice. very hip.
SnowAngel:	i considered borrowing chrissy's black coat with the faux fur trim, but decided it might be too much.
zoegirl:	especially since it's not all that cold out
SnowAngel:	what i really wanna borrow is maddie's bottle-cap belt. she took it back after the last time i wore it, tho, and i don't think i can call up and ask for it.
SnowAngel:	then again, who knows? maybe it'd be a good icebreaker.
zoegirl:	maybe
SnowAngel:	but nah, i'm not up for rejection right now. it would bum me out.
SnowAngel:	is it bad that i'm so excited while maddie's still so miserable?
zoegirl:	well, you're not excited BECAUSE she's miserable. they're too different things.
zoegirl:	you can't put your life on hold forever.
SnowAngel:	that's true
zoegirl:	but since the care package didn't work, maybe we

shld do something else to cheer her up. to give her a chance to come back.

SnowAngel:	only we've already given her lots of chances, and she hasn't taken any of them.
SnowAngel:	aye-yai-yai, it's 6:15 and everyone's meeting at the coffeehouse at 6:45. that's only half an hour away! *quick kiss and a hug for good luck* BYE!

Wed, Nov 17, 10:15 PM E.S.T.

SnowAngel:	well, i'm txting from my hot poetry date. NOT.
zoegirl:	uh oh. what's going on?
SnowAngel:	let's see, how should i put it?
SnowAngel:	BEN IS HERE WITH LESLIE. 😞
zoegirl:	who's leslie?
SnowAngel:	u remember! that GA state chick he's always talking about. the girl i convinced myself was just a friend.
zoegirl:	i take it she's not?
SnowAngel:	she's wearing a hideous pearl necklace, one that loops around twice and hangs down to her belly button!
SnowAngel:	why wld he go out with her when he could have ME?
zoegirl:	ah, angela
SnowAngel:	it's so unfair!
SnowAngel:	ew, now she's rubbing his neck. disgusting!!! 😖
zoegirl:	is the poetry slam itself any good? i mean, are you having ANY fun?
SnowAngel:	no.
SnowAngel:	ben read one of his poems—after prying himself away from leslie's claws—and it was BAD. it was about rebirth or resurrection or something, and i could tell from the way he read it that it was supposed to be really deep.
zoegirl:	but it wasn't?

SnowAngel:	at the end he pretended to be an egg. he scrunched into a ball with his arms wrapped around his legs and stayed like that, frozen, while everyone clapped.
zoegirl:	**oh good heavens**
SnowAngel:	my crush has been nipped in the bud. or, shall i say, my crush has been scrambled, fried, and poached. 🐣
SnowAngel:	tee-hee. that was funny, wasn't it?
zoegirl:	**at least you're in a good humor about it.**
SnowAngel:	well . . . maybe there's ONE good thing about tonight.
zoegirl:	**oh yeah?**
SnowAngel:	prepare yourself for another bombshell: doug schmidt is here.
zoegirl:	**doug schmidt? i didn't know he was in the drama club.**
SnowAngel:	he's not. he came on his own.
zoegirl:	**angela! did he come because he knew YOU were going to be there?**
SnowAngel:	how wld he have known i was going to be here?
SnowAngel:	no, he came to compete in the poetry slam—for real!
SnowAngel:	he read a poem about dirty underwear, which sounds gross, but it was really funny. UNLIKE mr. deep's stupid egg poem.
SnowAngel:	and afterward, he and i sat together and drank chai milkshakes while leslie caressed ben's hair. doug told me he wants to be a writer when he grows up, but that he would never take himself too seriously.
SnowAngel:	it was cool, cuz there's so much more to him than i thought.
zoegirl:	**so . . . where is he now? and is he your new crush?**

SnowAngel:	he left—and no!!! i have fun hanging out with him, but he is NOT my type.
zoegirl:	ha. like that's ever stopped you.
SnowAngel:	what r u implying? omg, u r so confusing sometimes!!!

Thu, Nov 18, 5:00 PM E.S.T.

SnowAngel:	i saw u talking to mr. h in the hall after 5th period, zo. he was looking VERY interested in what u had to say.
zoegirl:	we were talking about the quiz he gave in class. it was nothing.
SnowAngel:	well, he was rapt. have u figured out what ur gonna do about this weekend?
zoegirl:	aargh! i haven't! and every time i think about it, i get all jittery and i have to do jumping jacks to calm down.
SnowAngel:	ur gonna have to come up with something. time's a' tickin.
zoegirl:	i KNOW. he's expecting me at the kravitzes' TOMORROW NIGHT!!!
SnowAngel:	know who cld tell u what to do? maddie. she's always so good at cutting through the bullshit.
zoegirl:	i know. i NEED her, but how am i supposed to talk to her now that she's decided she's never going to talk to us???

Thu, Nov 18, 5:19 PM E.S.T.

zoegirl:	maddie, are you there?
zoegirl:	maddie, i need to talk to you. please?
zoegirl:	it's about mr. h.
zoegirl:	he wants me to go hot-tubbing with him, and i don't know what to do.
zoegirl:	maddie?
zoegirl:	ok. well, i really could have used your advice, but i guess you don't care!

zoegirl: i am so dead! i saw mr. h at fellowship this morning—i was too wimpy not to go—and when we were in the kitchen getting out the orange juice, he said, "i'm looking forward to tonight. i got a special candle just for the occasion."

SnowAngel: ew! ick, ick, ick!

zoegirl: he said it in this shy little boy way, and it would have been cute if i'd still been into him. but i'm not!!!

SnowAngel: did u tell him u couldn't come?

zoegirl: no! i said something brilliant like, "uh, great," and then i darted off to get a sweet roll—not that i was able to eat it. i wanted to tell him no, but i just couldn't!

SnowAngel: zoe, u have to get out of it.

zoegirl: how? he's coming to pick me up at seven. i already told my mom i'm going to Bible study with him, like years ago before i got freaked out, and she's delighted. she'll probably have a plate of cookies for him when he arrives.

SnowAngel: what if u told her the truth?

zoegirl: are you KIDDING? that would be a disaster. she'd call the entire school board, and then she'd realize i'd been lying to her all this time and she'd—crap, i have no idea what she'd do.

zoegirl: but it would be BAD!

SnowAngel: maybe u could get sick?

zoegirl: i suck at faking stuff. you know that.

SnowAngel: it's cuz ur such a goody-goody. u haven't had enough practice.

SnowAngel: maybe u could just not be there when he comes to pick u up?

zoegirl: where would i be, in a closet? anyway, there's still the mom problem because she knows i've got plans with him. i can't just disappear.

SnowAngel: i could

zoegirl: well, i can't!

zoegirl: my stomach's in knots. i keep imagining these horrible scenarios with the two of us alone in the kravitzes' hot tub. what do i do if he actually tries something?

SnowAngel: u say, "no!" and if he KEEPS trying, u slap his face and say, "no means no, u weirdo stalkerhead!"

zoegirl: thank you, that's very helpful.

SnowAngel: or i know! u could say, "now, now. what would jesus do?"

zoegirl: stop joking!

SnowAngel: i'm sorry. it's just that now I'M all anxious, and i don't know what else to do!

zoegirl: great. this is just great.

SnowAngel: shit, must put phone away. mr. kirk coming. something about some dude named shakespeare. only i don't know any dudes named shakespeare!

Fri, Nov 19, 7:05 PM E.S.T.

SnowAngel: MADDIE, I NEED TO TALK TO U! THIS IS SERIOUS!!!

SnowAngel: i know yr reading these texts, or i really THINK u r, so i'm gonna tell u anyway. i just got off the phone with zoe, and i'm totally flipping out.

SnowAngel: she's on her way to greg kravitz's house with mr. h— the kravitzes r out of town, it's a long story—and mr. h thinks that zoe is gonna go hot-tubbing with him.

SnowAngel: he showed up at the door while we were talking, and maddie, her voice got all panicky and she hung up really quick. WE HAVE TO DO SOMETHING!!!

SnowAngel: maddie!!! we're talking about zoe, who can't say

	no to anyone. straight-A honor student, ppl-pleasing zoe. do u understand how serious this is?
SnowAngel:	fine, i'll just figure something out myself. only i have no idea what to do and i can't stop thinking about it and if u were really her friend u'd help me. IF ANYTHING HAPPENS, HER BLOOD WILL BE ON YOUR SHOULDERS!!!
mad maddie:	**her blood will be on my SHOULDERS? god, ur dramatic.**
SnowAngel:	maddie! *weeps with gladness*
SnowAngel:	thank god!
mad maddie:	**anywayz, her blood would be on my HANDS, not dripping down my shoulders. why wld her blood be on my *shoulders*?**
SnowAngel:	whatever. what r we gonna do?
mad maddie:	**u said they're going to the kravitzes'?**
SnowAngel:	uh huh
mad maddie:	**then so r we. i'll pick u up in ten minutes.**
SnowAngel:	yes yes yes!
mad maddie:	**and grab your swimsuit. dunno about u, but i'm in the mood to go hot-tubbing.**

Sat, Nov 20, 10:35 AM E.S.T.

SnowAngel:	hi, dear, sweet maddie 😊
mad maddie:	**hi, angela**
SnowAngel:	have i told u how awesome u r yet this morning?
mad maddie:	**not unless u airmailed it.**
SnowAngel:	well, u r. *warm fuzzies for the mads, queen of heroic rescues*
mad maddie:	**whatevs**
mad maddie:	**we pulled it off, tho, huh?**
SnowAngel:	hell yeah! i keep seeing mr. h's face when we came through the back gate. how he went from

shocked to scared to "i'm cool, i'm cool" in, like, five
seconds.

mad maddie: **it was classic**

SnowAngel: and zoe!

SnowAngel: how her eyes were total saucers, especially when u
stepped into the hot tub in that hideous purple tank.

mad maddie: **i ordered it from j.crew last summer, but i never
wore it cuz it's so ugly.**

SnowAngel: it made u look like a bruise

mad maddie: **well i, for one, had a marvelous time. so nice,
lounging in a hot tub in the middle of november.**

SnowAngel: oh yes, we should do it more often.

mad maddie: **i'll mention it to mr. h. maybe we can squeeze
something in next weekend.**

SnowAngel: hahahahaha! the winsome threesome strikes again!
😎

SnowAngel: i say we go to shoney's breakfast bar to celebrate.
u game?

mad maddie: **well . . .**

SnowAngel: mmm, bacon. mmm, those fiendishly good french
toast sticks.

mad maddie: **ok, u convinced me**

SnowAngel: *pirouettes gleefully*

mad maddie: **u gonna text zoe?**

SnowAngel: u do it

mad maddie: **why me?**

SnowAngel: u know why. last night was all razzle-dazzle and
hysteria—and it was glorious—but i could tell there
was still weirdness b/w u two. zoe loves u and u luv
zoe, but u need to officially clear the air.

mad maddie: **oh, plz**

SnowAngel: r u scared?

mad maddie: **no, i'm not scared. god.**

so u'll do it, then. atta girl!

mad maddie: whatevs. i'll pick u up in half an hour!

Sat, Nov 20, 11:04 AM E.S.T.

mad maddie: hey, zo. it's me, maddie.

mad maddie: well, duh. obviously it's me, unless someone stole my phone.

zoegirl: maddie!!!! i was just going to call you!

mad maddie: yeah, sure

zoegirl: what do you mean? i was!

mad maddie: if u say so. so . . . what's up?

zoegirl: nothing much. i just wanted to thank you again. for last night.

mad maddie: tell me about it. i saved your butt good didn't i? i can't believe u let yourself be alone with him—and in a HOT TUB no less.

zoegirl: maddie!

zoegirl: i tell you thanks and your response is to tell me how stupid i was?

mad maddie: u have to admit u were. what the hell were u thinking?

zoegirl: i don't know what i was thinking!

zoegirl: anyway, i would think that you of all people would understand.

mad maddie: huh? what is THAT supposed to mean?

mad maddie: i think that *you* of all ppl would be grateful for being rescued! i wasn't that lucky, but U were!

zoegirl: stops.

zoegirl: breathes.

zoegirl: oh my gosh. why are we doing this?

mad maddie: honestly? i have no idea.

mad maddie: angela said things were weird between us, and i guess she was right.

zoegirl:	i guess so
mad maddie:	**fine**
zoegirl:	fine
mad maddie:	**FINE!**
zoegirl:	FINE!
zoegirl:	this is ridiculous.
mad maddie:	**so why don't u stop?**
zoegirl:	why don't U?
mad maddie:	**ok, i'm outta here**
zoegirl:	wait!
mad maddie:	**what?**
zoegirl:	thank you. i DO mean it.
zoegirl:	it's just that you must think i'm so pathetic.
mad maddie:	**i'm listening**
zoegirl:	because . . . you know. because it was all so awful. because i was, like, paralyzed, just sitting there clenching my toes while mr. h kept inching his way toward me. you would have never have let something like that happen.
mad maddie:	**uh, no, i'd just whip off my shirt instead. IF there were a hundred drunk frat boys there to appreciate it.**
zoegirl:	agh
zoegirl:	what is WRONG with us?
mad maddie:	**i have no idea**
zoegirl:	i am so embarrassed, maddie. 🌚
mad maddie:	**join the club**
zoegirl:	you know what? maybe i need a little bit of you— like your "screw u" ballsiness—and you need a little bit of me, like my lame scaredy-cat-ness. only in a good way (if that is possible).
mad maddie:	**you're not a lame scaredy-cat.**
zoegirl:	oh?

mad maddie:	well, maybe last night u were.
mad maddie:	but unlike me, u never would have screwed up so royally at that frat party. and NOT cuz u would have been scared, but just cuz u don't get sucked in by the whole popularity game.
mad maddie:	and that's great! don't get me wrong! but it's one of the reasons i felt so stupid about what happened, cuz i knew u were thinking u were so much better than me.
zoegirl:	no i wasn't! we *all* make mistakes—obviously.
mad maddie:	hmmm
mad maddie:	no comment
zoegirl:	why wouldn't you talk to us about it? we were totally there for you, but it's like you didn't want us.
mad maddie:	i DIDN'T, at first, cuz i was so pissed. and then the more time that went by, the harder it got.
mad maddie:	it just sucked, basically.
zoegirl:	it sucked for us too
zoegirl:	and i know i already told you this, but i AM sorry that angela and i talked about you behind your back.
zoegirl:	but honestly, we didn't mean to.
mad maddie:	i know. i'm sorry for overreacting.
zoegirl:	it's okay. i'm sorry for not being a better friend!
mad maddie:	should we be like playing violins and shit? angela would be bawling her eyes out.
zoegirl:	and you're not? kidding!
mad maddie:	speaking of angela, what would we throw in from her? if we were creating the perfect mix of the three of us, that is.
zoegirl:	i don't know. her love of makeup?
mad maddie:	her love of boys?
zoegirl:	her love of . . . what's that drama guy's name? her love of schlankers?

mad maddie: ZOE! i can't believe u said that!

zoegirl: see? i'm not such a saint.

mad maddie: i'd say u proved that last night, sister.

zoegirl: *covers head*

zoegirl: noooo! i don't want to think about it!

zoegirl: i'm just teasing about angela, though. you know i love her.

mad maddie: and you know i do too. and she loves us, and maybe that's what part of her we'd add in—her complete and full loyalty to her besties.

zoegirl: ♥

zoegirl: and fine, i admit it. it *was* pretty awesome when you two showed up last night.

mad maddie: yeah?

zoegirl: how you strolled through the kravitzes' back gate, gabbing about what a fabulous night it was for hot-tubbing?

mad maddie: heh heh heh

zoegirl: omigosh, and when you dropped down between me and mr. h, stretching out your legs and taking up as much room as possible? i about died.

mad maddie: just doing my duty, ma'am

zoegirl: you were practically in his lap!

mad maddie: AND he was wearing a speedo, which made it doubly horrific.

mad maddie: shit, zoe, what r u gonna do when u c him on monday?!!

zoegirl: i have no idea

mad maddie: what is HE gonna do?

zoegirl: i *seriously* have no idea

zoegirl: i wish i could switch out of his class, but i know it's impossible.

mad maddie: cldn't u get your mom to request it?

zoegirl: and tell her WHAT?

mad maddie:	ah. good point.
mad maddie:	at least u won't have to waste your time with that religious crap anymore.
zoegirl:	it wasn't the church's fault. i LIKED the church.
mad maddie:	oh, lord
zoegirl:	but i'm not worried about that. i'm worried about HIM.
mad maddie:	well, we'll figure something out together, u and me and angela. cuz, u know, all three of us r such pros when it comes to guys.
zoegirl:	yeah, right
zoegirl:	so whatever happened with ian? did you straighten things out with him?
mad maddie:	i've only seen him once since halloween, and that was last saturday when we worked together. at first he was all aloof, but we were thrown together so much that it was pretty much impossible NOT to talk.
zoegirl:	are you too a thing again, then?
mad maddie:	i wouldn't say we're a "thing." i'd say we're a "maybe." i didn't tell him exactly what happened on halloween night, but he knows i ditched him for jana, and he wasn't exactly thrilled.
zoegirl:	i can see that
zoegirl:	and speaking of, what about jana? are you going to patch things up?
mad maddie:	u have to ASK?
mad maddie:	u and angela were right—jana's a bitch. case closed.
zoegirl:	oh. well, sorry. except also—good!
mad maddie:	let's drop it. she's not worth talking about.
zoegirl:	you're so right
zoegirl:	here's a thought. if things work out with you and

	ian, then you two could double-date with angela and doug. (hee, hee)
mad maddie:	**angela and doug? as in doug schmidt?**
zoegirl:	the one and only
mad maddie:	**what happened to the schlank-master?**
zoegirl:	geez, ur behind the times. this is what u get when u drop off the face of the earth for two weeks.
mad maddie:	**fine, i guess i deserved that.**
zoegirl:	angela hung out with doug at a coffeehouse the other night, and i guess they had a really good conversation. she CLAIMS she's not going to start crushing on him, but you know angela.
mad maddie:	**good grief. will the madness ever stop?**
mad maddie:	**GOD it's good to talk to u. seriously, the last two weeks have been hell. without u and angela, i didn't know who i was anymore.**
zoegirl:	you're maddie, that's who. madigan kinnick, who swoops in like wonder woman to rescue me from sex-crazed english teachers, and who thinks up terrific ideas that angela or i would never come up with, like taking a road trip to cumberland island.
zoegirl:	are we still on???
mad maddie:	**u mean u still want to?**
zoegirl:	of course, you goof!
mad maddie:	**what about your parents?**
zoegirl:	what about them? as far as they know, the trip was never off. is that a problem?
mad maddie:	**no! it's just that i never thought**
mad maddie:	**i mean, i just assumed**
zoegirl:	what, that angela and i would let u bail on what's bound to be the most exciting thanksgiving vacation of our lives?

mad maddie: ah, crap. now i really am getting teary, can u believe it? i can't believe i'm getting teary over this.

zoegirl: we've GOT to call angela. she would kill us if she missed this historic moment.

mad maddie: crap again! angela! i'm supposed to pick her up so we can go to shoney's breakfast bar!

zoegirl: who's "we"?

mad maddie: *facepalm*

mad maddie: all three of us, of course

zoegirl: all three of us meaning you, angela, and me? yay!

mad maddie: wh-hoo!

zoegirl: but before we stop texting—does this mean things r good between us again?!

mad maddie: totally

zoegirl: thank goodness. i'm glad.

mad maddie: it's funny how some things r easier to say thru texting, isn't it?

zoegirl: but other things—like our road trip—are much more exciting to talk about in person. so get off your butt and come get me!

mad maddie: right on. to shoney's, my comrade!

zoegirl: talk to u soon!!!

FOLLOW THE WINSOME
THREESOME INTO
JUNIOR YEAR! TURN THE
PAGE FOR A PEEK AT

THE NEXT BOOK IN THE
INTERNET GIRLS SERIES!

SnowAngel:	hey there, zoe-cakes. r we studs or what? 😃
zoegirl:	yahootie!
SnowAngel:	i have a total adrenaline buzz going, even tho i am completely and thoroughly exhausted. my muscles r gonna be crazy sore tomorrow.
zoegirl:	i hear you. can you imagine how in shape we'd be if we did that every day?
SnowAngel:	we could call it the winsome-threesome workout-of-the-century. we cld make an exercise video and rake in oodles of cash.
zoegirl:	even my toenails are tired
SnowAngel:	*flops onto pretend bed and groans*
SnowAngel:	i told chrissy what we did, and she was like, "u ran up the escalator at peachtree center? that super-duper long one?"
zoegirl:	okay, yes but the critical point is that we ran up the *down* escalator. you did explain that to her, didn't u?
zoegirl:	that's gotta be the longest escalator in the world. seriously, it's as long as a football field.
SnowAngel:	i nearly lost it when maddie stopped for a breather and the escalator took her down, down, down. she was all, "noooo! i'm losing ground!"
zoegirl:	hee hee
SnowAngel:	but in the end we conquered it, cuz we can do ANYTHING, baby.
SnowAngel:	it's like in "the cave" by my buds Mumford & Sons. "but i will hold on hope . . . and i'll find strength in pain!"
zoegirl:	god, i love Mumford & Sons.
SnowAngel:	i know. and that one particular song—it's like therapy every time i listen to it.

zoegirl:	i like the line about wanting to live life as it's meant to be lived.
SnowAngel:	i do too, and how even when things are hard, we just keep going.
SnowAngel:	and do u know HOW we keep going? or at least how *i* keep going?
zoegirl:	how?
SnowAngel:	cuz of u and mads. ☺ ☺ ☺
zoegirl:	awwwww
SnowAngel:	it's true. true blue, me and u, and don't forget to add maddie 2.
SnowAngel:	do u like my rhyme?
zoegirl:	very impressive
SnowAngel:	wait, there's more! er, let's c . . . since 7th grade they did not part, they stayed connected in their hearts. zoe's the good girl, maddie's wild, and sweet darling angela is meek and mild.
zoegirl:	meek? hahahahaha! mild? hahahahaha!
SnowAngel:	fine, miss brainiac. U find something to rhyme with wild.
zoegirl:	"and sweet goofy angela tends to act like a child"?
SnowAngel:	hey now!
zoegirl:	just teasing. you know i love you.
zoegirl:	i've just got kid-type people on my brain, because guess what? i got the job at Kidding Around!
SnowAngel:	wh-hoo! *happy dance, happy dance*
zoegirl:	there was a message waiting for me when i got home. i'm psyched.
SnowAngel:	ah, what joy, to be wiping noses and chasing toddlers. when do u start?
zoegirl:	um, don't freak, okay?
SnowAngel:	why would i freak? ur not gonna say something to make me freak, r u?

SnowAngel:	wait a minute. don't u DARE tell me u have to start tonight.
zoegirl:	the thing is . . . i do.
SnowAngel:	zoe! noooo!
zoegirl:	saturday night's their busiest night! the director wants me to come in for training.
SnowAngel:	but we were gonna watch "Bridesmaids" again! and eat ugly carrots!
zoegirl:	i know, and i will miss eating my ugly carrot very much. but we can watch "Bridesmaids" tomorrow. that'll be even better, because that way maddie can join us.
SnowAngel:	the point being that she has plans tonight too? yeah, rub it in. u've got yr job and maddie has her cousin's wedding and i have a big old pile of poop. thanks a lot.
zoegirl:	angela, you are such a drama queen. and you don't have a big old pile of 💩. you have a delicious bag of carrots! with hopefully at least one ugly one mixed in for luck!
SnowAngel:	😦
zoegirl:	you're not really mad, are you?
SnowAngel:	of course i'm mad! *flames shoot from ears*
SnowAngel:	only not really, cuz this way i can watch as many episodes of "extreme makeover: home edition" as i want, and i will cry and it will be very emotional. if u would just TRY the show then u would c what i mean.
zoegirl:	umm . . . no
zoegirl:	but you know what's weird? and i mean this in the nicest way ever. last year you would have been totally upset if i'd changed our plans at the last minute. i mean, truly upset, with all kinds of

	wounded hurt feelings. but this year, you're so much more chill. why is that, do you think?
SnowAngel:	cuz i'm a junior, that's why. *struts around in funky junior-ness* cuz i can drive, even tho i don't have a car. cuz i choose to live my life the way it's meant to be lived, even tho i will be all alone on a saturday night, and even tho there is seriously something up with my parents, not that they'll admit it.
zoegirl:	there's something up with your parents? explain.
SnowAngel:	it's just this feeling i've been getting.
zoegirl:	like what? and for how long?
SnowAngel:	i dunno, maybe a week?
zoegirl:	a week?! why are you just now telling me???
SnowAngel:	it's like they're hiding something, i can't explain it better than that. i keep thinking that maybe i'm making it up, but then i think that i'm not.
zoegirl:	hmm
zoegirl:	maybe it's a *good* thing they're hiding—like that they're taking you to hawaii
SnowAngel:	i dunno, that somehow doesn't seem very likely.
SnowAngel:	but, whatever. i'm not gonna worry about it, cuz i'm the new and improved Chill Angela. u think they wld name a Barbie after me?
zoegirl:	definitely. for her accessory, she could have a tiny iPhone.
SnowAngel:	no, her accessory would be a tiny picture of u, me, and mads, cuz that's why i'm chill for real. cuz no matter what, i've got u guys giving me my me-ness.
zoegirl:	maddie and i don't give you your you-ness. you give yourself your you-ness.
SnowAngel:	"you-ness." now there's a word for ya.
SnowAngel:	my granddad's name was eunice, btw
zoegirl:	your granddad? don't you mean your grandmom?
SnowAngel:	nope, my granddad. only he spelled it "unus."

zoegirl: ugh. what were his parents trying to do to him?

SnowAngel: his full name was unus faye. he went by U.F.

zoegirl: i am so sorry to hear that.

SnowAngel: yep

zoegirl: well, on that note, gtg. wish me luck on my first
               day, which is really my first night!

SnowAngel: good luck on yr first day which is really ur first night!

SnowAngel: ta ta for now!

Why were your books banned and do you personally believe that they should have been?

Lots of my books have teen girls in them. Teen girls sometimes talk about sex. Teen girls sometimes have sex. Lots of grown-ups would like to believe that this is not true. I am not one of those grown-ups, and I think it's important and meaningful to give readers stories that reflect reality—in a respectful way. Like, not salaciously, but with the intent of saying, "Let's look at how this story played out. How'd it seem to work out for so-and-so?" And then the readers—who are SMART, damn it—can grapple with those issues themselves. And no, I do not believe my books should have been banned. I do not believe that any author should be banned, ever. Freedom of speech, dude. :)

What's your response when you are censored? Are you ever frustrated, or do you take pride in it?

At first I cried. And called my editor and apologized, because I felt so terrible about it. Now I take pride . . . but it requires a bit of emotional effort, because it still hurts to have people say, out loud and with venom, "Your books suck. YOU suck."

What was your favorite part of writing the Internet Girls series?

My fave part of writing this series was NOT HAVING TO WRITE SETTING. I hate setting. In other books that aren't purely written in text/IMs, my annoying (awesome) editor makes me include setting, and it is hard.

Which of your characters is most like you, and which character do you wish you were more like?

I'm most like Winnie from the Winnie Years series. She's a good girl, funny, tries to do the right thing. Often gets into embarrassing situations. I once ran over a squirrel on my bike.

Whom do I wish I were more like? I'm going to go with Cat from *Shine*, because she has courage in spades. She doesn't let the haters get to her. Sometimes I do.

How do you come up with your characters?
I follow my children around as they go through their lives and I spy on them. I wear a trench coat and carry a notepad. I am vair vair subtle.

Except, really, I do.

As an author, what's your average day like?
Oh, an average day of writing means MAKING MYSELF WRITE. And then thinking, "Oh, this is fun." And then writing some more.

What do you think books offer that other forms of entertainment don't?
Books engage readers in a more intimate way than other forms of entertainment/media, I think. They encourage critical thinking.

What is your very best life advice?
Best advice? Sheesh. Imagine life is like this: You're waiting at a red light. You're stuck there. You didn't choose to be, but there you are. How are you going to spend your time? Bitching and moaning and looking at your watch, or thinking INTERESTING thoughts? Looking at the beautiful sky? Laughing at a joke? So, use this life WISELY—we're dead a lot longer than we're alive—and leave the universe a better place than when you got here.

ACKNOWLEDGMENTS

Thanks to my informants—er, *consultants*—Sarah Chesney and Laura Chaddock, for helping me with the form. Thanks to Jack, Laura, Suzy, Julianne, Mag, and Gin for giving me great advice on the story itself. And finally, a special Angela-style thank you to my editor, Susan Van Metre, whose idea this novel was in the first place: Wh-hoo! We did it! *SUPERFLYINGTACKLEPOUNCE*

ABOUT THE AUTHOR

LAUREN MYRACLE is the author of many books for teens and young people, including the *New York Times* bestselling Internet Girls series, *Shine*, *Rhymes with Witches*, *Bliss*, *The Infinite Moment of Us*, and the Flower Power series. She lives with her family in Fort Collins, Colorado. Visit her online at laurenmyracle.com.